CLUES TO THE EXCITEMENT ABOUT THREE-TIME EDGAR AWARD–NOMINEE ROBERT BARNARD

THE SKELETON IN THE GRASS "IS IN FACT A SPLENDID MAINSTREAM NOVEL EXPLORING A THEME THAT LINKS ALL GOOD MYSTERIES WITH THE LARGER LITERARY TRADITION: THE BURDEN OF THE PAST. . . . BARNARD'S NARRATIVE NEVER LOSES ITS TIGHT FOCUS ON A DOMESTIC WORLD AS RICHLY EVOKED AS IN ANYTHING BY GALSWORTHY OR TROLLOPE."
—*Time*

"THE WRIEST WIT AND MOST SCATHING SATIRE IN TODAY'S MYSTERY." —*Chicago Sun-Times*

"BARNARD [HAS] AN EYE FOR THE SELF-DELUSION AND HYPOCRISY IN ALL OF US . . . and the result is a growing series of mysteries that are entertaining . . . quite funny . . . and acutely observing." —*The Boston Globe*

"THERE'S NO ONE QUITE LIKE ROBERT BARNARD in his ability to combine chills and chuckles and then sprinkle the whole with delicious irony."
— *The San Diego Union*

BY THE SAME AUTHOR

At Death's Door
The Cherry Blossom Corpse
Bodies
Political Suicide
Fête Fatale
Out of the Blackout
Corpse in a Gilded Cage
School for Murder
The Case of the Missing Brontë
A Little Local Murder
Death and the Princess
Death by Sheer Torture
Death in a Cold Climate
Death of a Perfect Mother
Death of a Literary Widow
Death of a Mystery Writer

THE
Skeleton
IN THE
Grass

—— • ——

Robert Barnard

A DELL BOOK

Published by
Dell Publishing
a division of
Bantam Doubleday Dell Publishing Group, Inc.
666 Fifth Avenue
New York, New York 10103

For information address: Charles Scribner's Sons, New York, New York.

The trademark Dell ® is registered in the U.S. Patent and Trademark Office.

ISBN: 0-440-20327-9

Reprinted by arrangement with Charles Scribner's Sons

Printed in the United States of America

May 1989

10 9 8 7 6 5 4 3 2 1

OPM

I

———— ● ————

A sudden chill breeze from the river caught Sarah as she leant through her bedroom window. She drew her cardigan around her, wishing it wasn't a fawn cardigan— wondering, indeed, whether a cardigan was the sort of garment you wore at a house like Hallam. Mummy had always been very insistent on cardigans: they were to be worn in all except the hottest of weathers. Here they seemed drab and utilitarian, particularly ones in fawn (Mummy's choice).

Sarah's bedroom had been distinctly grander than she had expected, and she didn't feel quite comfortable in it yet. The bed was a solid structure, the furniture good and abundant. Only a slight air of mustiness had made her open the window. But Sarah knew that these old houses always had hanging over them a light shroud of must.

Out on the lawn the family seemed to be gathering for tea. She had seen Mr. Hallam come out from his study, still carrying a book, the one she had seen him reading when she had been taken in to be introduced. Now Pinner the manservant was bringing out a collapsible table, the dog playing around his feet. Mrs. Hallam and Elizabeth were already there, one sewing, the other reading, in a companionable peace that Sarah had never managed to achieve with her own mother. She wondered whether Mrs. Hallam really expected her to join them. She had said so, certainly, but it had seemed an odd invitation to give to a new nursemaid-cum-governess. Except that Mrs. Hallam had stressed that she was *not* to be that: was a friend and helper with whom little Chloe was to grow up. Yes, on consideration it did seem as if Mrs. Hallam expected her to go down to tea on the lawn. Perhaps it would be better to go before the sons arrived. To walk across the lawn under too many strange gazes would be an ordeal best avoided.

In spite of that occasional breeze the sun seemed to be quite hot. It was, after all, July. Sarah decided not to wear her cardigan, but in an unconscious obeisance to her mother she folded it up neatly and put it away in the drawer for woollens. Then she patted her hair before the long mirror inside her wardrobe, and went out into the bewildering maze of corridors.

For Hallam seemed, this first time she was alone in it, all dark wood panelling and irregular corridors. As long as she kept to them she knew she could not be intruding on anybody, but when she had descended the broad, in-timidating staircase—lightened by a modern portrait that she thought must be of Mrs. Hallam—she found herself in the square, oak-panelled hallway which she had been impressed by when she had arrived. The main door to the house was certainly not the one she should use to get to the garden, but which of the rooms should she go through to find that side entrance? Fortunately Sarah had a well-developed sense of direction, and the second door she tried revealed a booklined sitting-room, at the far end of which she saw a door—a post-Elizabethan addition—that led out to the lawns. Nervously she tried it, and stepped out into the little terraced garden. She dallied through its prettiness, but there was no avoiding the walk across the lawn, and when she had embarked upon it she found it every bit as difficult as she had feared. The expanse was so huge, and so exposed, for it only gained a softening of trees as it sloped down to the river. How, even in flat, sensible shoes, could one walk naturally? What did one do with one's arms? Did one *smile?* And if one couldn't smile all the way over, how did one contrive to look agreeable and contented?

But when she finally approached the little group, Mrs. Hallam behaved perfectly, as Sarah had known she would.

"Sarah! How nice. Just in time. I won't be silly and ask if you've made yourself at home, because I know it will be some time before Hallam is anything like home to you. But being unpacked and settled in is something, isn't it?"

Elizabeth had smiled a brief but friendly smile, and Mr. Hallam had taken his pipe out and patted an empty deckchair. But it was Mrs. Hallam who was responsible for that surge of warmth in Sarah that she recognized as something close to love. She was so beautiful, there in the sunlight: her pale auburn hair drawn back; the oval face, the slim, graceful body that one could hardly believe had borne four children, the first more than twenty years before. And her beauty was not a cool sort of loveliness, but warm, concerned. She was a woman who made herself loved.

"And such a confusing house it is, too," she was saying. "Rambling isn't the word for it. Positively maze-like. But I've never known any Tudor house that was anything clsc."

"But Sarah was brought up in a vicarage, wasn't

she?" said Mr. Hallam, looking up from his book with interrogative eyebrows. "Most of them are pretty large and warrenlike."

"Actually ours is quite small," said Sarah, her voice coming out as a little squeak. "It is a poor parish."

Small. And cold. And with that little worm of meanness and ill-temper at its heart. Her father.

"Ah yes—it is in Derbyshire, isn't it? That's where you were brought up? And did the munificence of the Dukes of Devonshire not extend to your parish?"

"Oh no. We are well outside their sphere of influence. Though my father was invited to Chatsworth once."

"Now *there's* a house. I reviewed a book on Chatsworth and the Dukes of Devonshire last year. I seem to remember I came down hard on the old boys' sense of *noblesse oblige*, but some of them were really rather endearing old birds."

Sarah nodded intelligently, thankful that she knew quite a lot about the Dukes of Devonshire. It was really quite thrilling to hear Mr. Hallam talk about books. The Hallams of Hallam had a certain local fame, and it had even penetrated as far as Derbyshire: when Sarah had applied for the job her mother had heard of them, and had contributed a few details about the family's history. But it was the reviewing, the weekly column in the *Observer,* that had made Dennis Hallam's name a household word—at any rate in intellectual and politically aware households. The reviews were urbane, witty, learned—or on occasion trenchant and almost Swiftian in their scorn for time-servers, muddled thinkers, or those on the make. The subjects that moved him were cruelty, war, and the destruction of the British heritage. She knew he was a great campaigner for the League of Nations, and had lent his fervour and his handsome presence to meetings up and down the country. His promotion of the League's aims had led to trouble, frequently, with Fascist mobs. She knew too that he had been wounded in the Great War—and she suspected that the scars were as much mental as bodily.

"Ah, here are the sandwiches," said Mrs. Hallam. "They look lovely. I'll go and fetch the cake, Mrs. Munday."

"Bless you, madam—a cream cake out in this heat?" said the cook, who was ample in that way that Sarah had always imagined country house cooks ought to be. "That'd do it no good at all. I'll bring it out when you've done with the sandwiches."

"You are kind. Oh good—here's Oliver coming." Mrs. Hallam smiled at the approach of her elder son. "I don't think we can expect Will. He's busy conspiring with one of his friends in his room."

"I fear the boy will be a politician," said Dennis Hallam, with a sceptical smile.

"Shall I take the boys something?" asked Mrs. Munday.

"No, certainly not," said Mrs. Hallam. "If they want tea they can come out here and have it with us. Ah, Oliver: this is Sarah. Come to help with Chloe."

Oliver, the heir to Hallam, was inclined to be plump, though certainly he could not yet be called fat. He had a kind, comfortable smile, and an air of being intelligent without being an intellectual. He had travelled and worked in the Middle East after school, and was now about to begin his Finals year at Oxford. He greeted Sarah pleasantly, and sank into a chair.

"Will is solving the unemployment problem with public works," he said, "and undermining the Nazi government through a network of *agents provocateurs*. By tomorrow we shall either see a Red Dawn, or the end of civilization as we know it."

The tea was wonderful, Sarah thought. There were cucumber sandwiches, of course, and sandwiches with what she decided must be relish, and a variety of others made with what Mrs. Munday must have had around in the kitchen, all of them cut so delicately and presented so imaginatively that the everyday became a treat. No crusts to be eaten up, either—Sarah's childhood had been dominated by crusts to be eaten up, and waste not want not. Only the cream cake, when Mrs. Munday brought it, seemed to Sarah excessively rich—but then she had been frugally brought up, and the Hallam children hadn't: they tucked into it with a will, especially Oliver. Red squirrels darted over the lawn from tree to tree, and Bounce, the Hallam retriever, chased anything that moved with an amiable determination not to catch it. The conversation ranged over books and politics and personal concerns, and sometimes Mr. Hallam talked quietly to Sarah about her background, and the doings in her father's parish. This last subject was a little embarrassing. Sarah could say nothing about her father's alienation from his flock—by his lack of vocation, his meanness, his petty rages—but she said something about his "difficulties."

"I can imagine," said Dennis Hallam. "People talk about changes in country life, even a revolution, but they don't know what they are talking about. The changes are only skin-deep, and at the heart there's the same darkness and superstition that there always was. I'm afraid we are quite alien here. They look up to us because we are the family at the big house—which is the last thing we'd want. But if I talk to them about the things that really concern me, I meet a wall of dogged, dumb resistance. I expect your father finds the same."

"Something of it," admitted Sarah, conscious of meeting openness with reticence. "My mother gets through to the local people better. Perhaps Mrs. Hallam—does too."

"Oh, absolutely. Helen—please call her Helen. And I'm Dennis. But Helen only gets through to them on a domestic level, and only to the women. If she starts talking about the things we have close at heart—and she's as concerned about them as I, though she loathes public meetings—then she meets the same blank wall. Really we should live in town, though I only feel at peace in the country."

"You'd fit in in town, Father," broke in Oliver, "because there you'd find plenty of earnest, right-thinking citizens like yourself. If you talked to the char, or the man digging up the road outside your house, you'd find just the same resistance."

"A few like-minded souls wouldn't go amiss," said Dennis Hallam, with a wry smile. "At least they'd be an improvement on Cousin Mostyn—who for our sins we have to visit tomorrow."

"Not to mention Major Coffey, who will doubtless also be gracing the occasion," said Helen Hallam. "Though that odious man was hardly spawned by the countryside."

"Oh God," said Oliver. "Cousin Mostyn is one thing, but Coffey I can't abide. I think tomorrow will be devoted to concentrated revision of 18th-century history."

"How cowardly the young are," murmured Helen. "You'll come with us, won't you, Elizabeth?"

"If you want me to, Mummy. Sarah and I can go into the garden."

So it seemed assumed that she would go with them.

Oh dear. New people. So many new people at once, and she in that confusing, Jane Eyre-like position of being neither servant nor gentry. Sarah looked at the dappled lawn, the panting dog, the shimmering red-brick house in the distance, and felt conflicting emotions of peace and panic.

The peace was dissipated by a figure running from the house. It was a slim, boyish figure, in white shirt and grey flannels. His family kinship was proclaimed by his flaming hair—brilliant, where his mother's was delicate, almost peach-coloured. It flopped down over one eye, giving him an appearance at once schoolboyish yet vaguely piratical. He was racing across the lawn as if pursued by Furies.

"I've just heard!" he panted. "On the six o'clock news. Franco has raised the standard. There's civil war in Spain."

The news would have been received in the rectory in Derbyshire with a mild, disinterested curiosity. Perhaps her father would even have approved. Here the news met with strong and instant horror and outrage.

"Is it confirmed?"

"What is the government doing?"

"Has he landed on the mainland?"

"Will all the troops follow him?"

Dennis Hallam stood up.

"I must telephone the League of Nations Union chairman. We must press the government to get a strong motion through at Geneva. And they must follow it up with the threat of sanctions against anyone supporting Franco. I expect Mussolini is behind this. If only we could count on this spineless government of ours to take a determined line. Their instinct will be to stand heroically aside."

"Sanctions won't do any good," said Will scornfully. "This is war. This one we have to fight."

"But of course we're going to fight," said Dennis. "As I said, we'll press in Geneva—"

"I mean *fight*. I'm going to go there to fight."

There was a second's silence. It was clear to Sarah that they took him seriously.

"Don't be absurd, old chap," said Oliver.

"Will, darling, surely we've brought you up to believe —" began Helen Hallam.

"Oh, I know what I've been brought up to believe. Only I don't believe it any more."

"Will, dear old thing," said Dennis earnestly, "I know how one reacts at first to things like this: one wants to fight back. It's an almost irresistible urge. But one has to resist it! Fighting back never settled anything."

"Fighting back stopped the Spanish Armada," said Will, obviously clutching at the first historical example that came into his head. "What good have all your motions and resolutions done for Abyssinia? Did they stop Herr Hitler from marching into the Rhineland? They're just impotence with a loud voice."

"That's a very fine phrase, Will," said Dennis quietly. "But is that really all your mother's and my work means to you?"

Will looked momentarily shamefaced, and Helen said quickly:

"No, Dennis, you shouldn't put it like that. This is not a personal thing. The point is that if the governments of the world put their hearts into economic sanctions they really will work. And they'll work without the terrible, senseless slaughter we went through in the war."

"If, if, if," said Will impatiently. "But of course they won't put their heart into sanctions. Half of them will be hoping that Franco wins. Just watch Cousin Mostyn when you go to Cabbot Hall tomorrow. He'll be positively purring at the prospect. And he's in the government."

"Only at the most junior level," protested Oliver. "Even Mr. Baldwin would never appoint such a stumblebum to anything of any importance."

"The point is that there *is* no will to impose sanctions, so the only thing is to help the government of Spain to fight. I'm going to go to London tomorrow. Someone there will be getting things organized."

"You're not of age, Will," put in Elizabeth quietly.

"I'm of age to join the British Army. Nobody can stop me going to fight for Spain."

"It's not a question of trying to *stop* you," wailed Helen. "It's a question of trying to *convince* you."

"Will," said Dennis quietly, "I've told you this many times, and I'll tell you it again. Back in 1913 we got up a Hallam cricket team to play the village lads. Boys from houses around here, men who'd been with me at school and Oxford. After the match we all came back here to tea, stood on the turf you're standing on now. It was one of the happiest days of my life. In a year we were all at war. I was sent to Egypt. I came back with a gammy leg, and you were born. All the rest were sent to France and Flanders. In two years all but one were dead. Can you really say that giving the Kaiser a bloody nose was worth the decimation of the best of our young men?"

Will paused, in order to reply with becoming gravity.

"I don't say that it was. No, I don't think it was. But I do think there are *some* things one has to fight. I do think that if Herr Hitler invaded Britain I would fight, because there are some governments so disgusting that no one should be forced to live under them. I think Oliver would fight Hitler too, if it came to the pinch. I think Spain is the same sort of issue."

"Franco is just an old-fashioned martinet, under the thumb of the Church," protested Dennis.

"People should not have to live under him. And it's a question of defending democracy, defending the rule of law."

"And what makes you think that you will be any help in the fight?" asked Oliver sardonically. "You, who even refused to join the school cadet corps?"

Will flushed.

"Of course I'd be useless, now. But this isn't a fight that's going to be over in two or three months. I think it will last years. I shall train, and lots of people like me will train, and *then* we won't be useless."

And to cut off the argument he turned and ran back to the house, very fast. He seemed to do nothing except in extremes. Sarah felt she had never seen anyone so vital, so full of fire and purpose.

The tea-party was over. Dennis's review copy lay unregarded in his deckchair. Helen was dabbing her eyes.

"Don't worry, darling," said Dennis, putting his arm around her. "We'll stop him."

"We can't *stop* him. We've always brought our children up to make their own decisions."

"Probably the revolt will fizzle out in a week or two, or be crushed. I must telephone the chairman of the League of Nations Union . . ."

And the little party began trailing back towards the house, Dennis moving with his characteristic slight limp.

"Oh dear, Sarah," said Helen. "What must you think of us? And on your first day!"

A swallow swooped in front of Bounce, but he declined to pursue it. Over the lawn the shadows had lengthened, and nippy breezes came up from the river. Sarah wished she had brought her cardigan.

2

─────── ● ───────

By the next day Sarah found it was assumed among the Hallams that she would be going with them to Cousin Mostyn's. She would have preferred to stay behind, but it would have seemed ungrateful and unadventurous to say so. That Cousin Mostyn lived so close, she gathered, was not due to any family or property reasons, still less to any pull of affection; it was due merely to the fact that he was MP for the Oxfordshire constituency in which they all lived. Mostyn's "place" was called Cabbot Hall, and he had bought it when he had been elected, in 1931. "A dull house," said Dennis Hallam. He did not add, because he didn't need to: "and eminently suitable."

Sarah wondered what she was to do with little Chloe. "She can come with us, or stay with Mrs. Munday," said Helen. At first Sarah thought this a little unfair on Mrs. Munday, who no doubt had her own duties to do, and a dinner to cook, but when she saw the pair together she retracted her opinion: they clearly doted on each other.

Chloe was a sprite of a girl: fair-haired, lithe, active, she radiated glee and physical well-being. Forward for her six years, as was to be expected, she was also independent: she only demanded to "know" things when she had failed to work them out for herself. Standing with Helen, watching her as she played around the stables which were her great joy, Sarah was only conscious of an aura of gold, of dancing delight, of a joyous relish for life.

"She was an afterthought, of course," said Helen. "Or rather a lack of forethought."

Sarah blushed. Such frankness would have been unthinkable at the vicarage.

"But not the less loved for that," added Helen, seeing her embarrassment. "She is a love of a child."

Chloe debated long and seriously whether to go to Cabbot Hall or stay with Mrs. Munday. In the end she decided to stay, on the grounds that Bounce would otherwise be lonely. The family's sense of social responsibility clearly had descended to her. Sarah had her own debate, on what to wear, being very unsure what kind of occasion this was to be. By now she was friendly enough with Elizabeth to call her in, and she gave her opinion gravely, though both girls were conscious that Sarah's wardrobe hardly presented an infinity of choice.

The family's dilemma was over which car to take. The Wolseley was more comfortable, but the Austin Seven was more loved. Cousin Mostyn would be displeased, Dennis said, to see them arrive in so plebeian a car, especially as it was very dirty, and had had REDS scrawled in its dust by some village lout, presumably in mistaken reference to their politics. When Chloe decided to stay at Hallam, and since Oliver was claiming his desperate need to revise eighteenth-century history, the choice of the Austin Seven became inevitable, in spite of the crush.

All the day's arguing and playfulness cloaked, as Sarah was well aware, the subject that was really preoccupying everybody. Will had gone to London by the first

train. Who he would see there, what he would do, nobody quite knew, for he had been busy packing and
telephoning the night before. They did not expect to get a
postcard from Madrid or Barcelona in the next few days,
but on the other hand they knew Will's fiery nature,
knew that he might commit himself impulsively to some
course of action, from which he would later find it impossible to back down. Oliver had phoned one or two of his
friends in London who he guessed might be involved in
any activity going on, but he got the impression that,
until the news from Spain became more definite, until
they knew that the government could put up a real resistance to the leaders of the revolt, much was being mooted
but little was being done. That, at any rate, was comfort.
Oliver emphasized to all these friends that his brother
was very young, was to go up to Oxford in October, and
that any decision he made to go and fight would be very
disturbing to his parents. He came back from these talks
with a conviction that there was a new, more aggressive
spirit abroad among the young, but he did not communicate this to his elders.

The gathering at Cousin Mostyn's, Sarah had discovered, was "drinks." Just drinks. They would be coming
home for dinner. Cousin Mostyn threw these modest parties periodically, according to Dennis to butter up his
middle-class constituents. He liked the Hallams to come
along, partly because they had both local and national
prestige, partly because their presence demonstrated his
broad-mindedness. "Which is no doubt why he also in-
vites Major Coffey," said Dennis dourly. "I at least pay
Mostyn the compliment of doubting that he is a Fascist."
So Major Coffey, apparently, was.

They left Hallam at about a quarter to six. Elizabeth
and Sarah climbed into the back seat, Sarah being very

careful not to crease her dress, and the older Hallams sat in the front, Dennis driving with a nonchalant expertise. Sarah decided it was a delightful little car—which was odd, because they had an Austin Seven at home, and she had never considered it in any other light than a means of getting from here to there. This car, however, which was called "Bumps," contained hidden delights: Will's cricket pads on the floor, a Jerusalem newspaper brought back by Oliver and stuffed down the side of the seat, items of make-up scattered by Helen, and at least three books sent to Dennis for review. It was a car, too, that seemed made to cruise through the country lanes, whereas the Wolseley would undoubtedly have seemed over-assertive, a Blenheim Palace among cars. Most of the countrymen they passed were too late realizing who the driver was to tip their caps to him. It was like being an ordinary family, out on a joy-ride.

When Helen pointed out Cabbot Hall in the middle distance Sarah saw what they meant when they described it as a dull house. A fine position, on a gentle rise, but a dull house. The architect had been handed an opportunity, and muffed it. It had been built in the 1790s, and it demonstrated only the tired clichés of the late Georgian style. It was quite modest in size, but then Cousin Mostyn was apparently quite modestly off, and he and his wife had no children.

Sarah was conscious, in making these judgements, that if she had had a friend in Derbyshire who lived in a house like this, she would have thought it quite tremendously grand.

They were by no means the first to arrive at Cabbot Hall, and Bumps was niftily inserted between cars both grander and cleaner. Sarah got out carefully, and was pleased to find her dress had not suffered greatly from the

squash, though she was upset to see a woman going up
the steps of the house who seemed to have dressed for a
Buckingham Palace garden party.

"She's the butcher's wife," murmured Helen. "So it
doesn't seem *too* unkind to talk about mutton dressed up
as lamb."

Inside, in the big, dull entrance hall, Mostyn Hallam
and his wife were greeting their guests. Mostyn, Sarah
had by now found out, was something very lowly in Mr.
Hore Belisha's Ministry of Transport. One of the family
jokes was that his nose had inspired the famous Belisha
Beacons. It was indeed a very red nose, but it was in a
very red face, suggesting high blood pressure and a delight in the pleasures of the table. He was portly, affable,
his voice slightly over-loud as he shook hands all round.
The over-dressed lady and her beefy but otherwise incon-
spicuous husband were just ahead of them.

"Ah, Mr. Fowler. Good to see you here again. And
your lovely lady wife. You look younger every time I see
you, my dear. You know everyone? I'm sure everyone
knows you. Fowler sells the best meat in Oxfordshire, so
I always say."

It seemed safe to assume that Mr. Fowler was the
only butcher invited to that particular shindig.

Cousin Mostyn was clearly pleased to see the other
Hallams. When Helen introduced Sarah she watched him
for any signs of displeasure that they had brought along
the nursery governess, but even her over-sensitivity could
discern nothing—mere friendliness, albeit of an avuncular kind.

"Ah—Sarah Causeley, come to look after little Chloe,
is that it? Bit of a handful, eh?"

"A very delightful handful, anyway," said Sarah.

"Oh, absolutely. Charming child."

At the mention of Chloe Sarah had seen a look of pain pass over Mrs. Mostyn Hallam's face. She was a well-groomed, well-dressed woman, who nevertheless contrived to present a vaguely washed-out appearance. It was easy to guess that the late arrival of Chloe, to the senior Hallams who already had three children, had been to her a matter of pain and reproach.

"Winifred, my wife," said Mostyn, waving. Sarah smiled, shook hands, and then they all moved on.

Sarah soon found that, if there were anomalies in her position at the gathering, there were anomalies in the occasion as a whole—as perhaps was inevitable, given that its purpose was political rather than social. People were forced into proximity whose normal contacts were no more than the transmitting of orders and the fulfilling of them. One could hardly use this opportunity to complain about the lamb Mr. Fowler had sent up last week, or the quality of the last batch of shirt-collars some other worthy tradesman had supplied. Instead there was a great deal of heartiness, of kind inquiries about health or children, and the weather was much mulled over.

Sarah felt no kinship with gentry or tradespeople. She thought that even a clergyman would be welcome, but there was none in sight. She felt closer to a young waiter, clearly hired for the occasion and not yet quite sure of the tricks of his trade, who approached her with a tray.

"A drink, miss?"

He was a chunky young man with a slight Oxfordshire burr and an amused eye.

"Yes, I think I would like one. But I'm not sure what to have."

"I think you'll find sherry quite a safe choice, miss."

He inclined the side of the tray with the sherries. She

smiled and he smiled. Then he was summoned by a horsey voice, and he moved off, his face impassive.

Everyone of importance seemed to have arrived, and Mostyn and Winifred Hallam began moving among their guests. Winifred was diligent in her inquiries after health and children, but she seemed to do it with more concern and more previous knowledge than most of her guests. This was no doubt a consequence of being a politician's wife. Mostyn was doling out "Trade's picking up" to the commercial interests, and "Weather's no good in your line" to the farmers—this last a safe bet, since even Sarah was aware that weather, for farmers, was invariably of the wrong sort.

At one point, as Mostyn passed regally by, Dennis Hallam took him by the arm and said in a friendly way:

"Some time, when the crush thins out, I'd like to have a word with you about Spain."

"Spain? Thinking of going there on holiday? Frightfully hot this time of year."

"Mostyn, civil war is breaking out there."

"Civil war? Oh no, I don't think so. Comic opera stuff. They go in for that kind of thing down there. Over in a week, you mark my words. Bang-bang, wave a few flags, and it's all over." He lowered his voice to something lower than a bellow, and assumed a conspiratorial stance that did indeed seem to derive from comic opera. "But I'll tell you something that will interest you . . ."

Everyone in the vicinity pricked up their ears, but Cousin Mostyn was sublimely unaware that he was being listened to.

"What's that?"

"The King's going on holiday. To the Aegean. And he's taking with him that American woman."

Dennis shrugged.

"I don't expect he'll send me a postcard."

"But you can't take it that lightly, old man! It's getting to be quite frightful. You've no idea what the American newspapers are saying."

"I can imagine."

"The Duff Coopers will be with them. But I never thought Duff entirely sound. And his ways with women . . ."

"I was at Oxford with Duff. I know all about his ways with women. But I thought the danger with the King was that he might want to marry this American woman."

"It is, old man, it is."

"If he follows Duff's example he'll go in quite the opposite direction."

"Well, let's damned well hope so . . ."

"But getting back to Spain—"

Sarah saw Elizabeth raising an eyebrow at her, and nodding in the direction of the garden. The two girls slipped through the morning-room towards the French windows. As they scurried along they heard one of the guests say, in a broad country accent:

"That weren't our King they was talkin' about, were it? Our King i'n't got no woman."

The fresh air was invigorating. The two girls sipped at their drinks and grinned at each other.

"Daddy is butting his head against a brick wall," said Elizabeth. "I sometimes think he prefers it that way. First Cousin Mostyn will say that there isn't going to be a war in Spain, then he'll say it's best left to the Spaniards —don't want to get involved with their squabbles, what? Then he'll say anyway the government was a bit red, wasn't it, far as he'd heard, and it might well be good riddance to bad rubbish, that's what a lot of fellers are saying around Westminster. It's much more difficult to argue with stupid people than with intelligent ones, and after all these years at meetings and discussion groups and study groups, Daddy has never realized that. Or rather, he treats everybody as if they were intelligent."

"Well, it's a nice trait," said Sarah. Then she added, in an unusual burst of confidence, "My father treats everyone as if they were fools."

"Oh dear. I wouldn't like that. Including you?"

"Much of the time. We're very used to it—Mummy and me, I mean . . . perhaps his problem is more with himself than with other people."

It was a piece of understanding of her father that came to her like a gift from the air. She felt she would never have realized it if she had not met the Hallams.

"Well, at least Daddy's fault is on the right side," said Elizabeth. "But one doesn't want to hear him battle it out with Cousin Mostyn, because one knows so well he will get nowhere . . . Oh golly, there's Fiona Macauley. She's going to ask me if I'm going to do the Season next year, and I really can't decide . . ."

"Why not?"

"Well, it will probably be a frightful bore, but there *are* all those gorgeous and unreliable chaps, and if one doesn't get to know all the bounders early on, one probably falls victim to them in middle age, and really they might be quite *fun* . . ."

"You go and talk to her. I'm quite happy roaming around in the garden. I love gardens more than anything in the world."

And Sarah wandered off. She liked Elizabeth, but found her somehow unformed. It was exciting in a way: she might turn out to be any number of different things— a campaigner, like her parents, a social butterfly, a perfectly ordinary wife and mother. Perhaps the same is true

of me, Sarah thought, and then decided it was probably
not. She, at any rate, had no desire to "do the Season,"
and thought it would probably be a crushing bore to anyone as intelligent as Elizabeth, and the young men much
less fun than she wistfully imagined. But talk of it merely
emphasized that there were areas where their lives were
so different as barely to touch. Besides, Sarah was a girl
who preferred the company of men: she knew that her
life would centre on men, not in any courtesan way, but
in a companionate one—they being the people with the
interesting lives. Sarah intended that her life should be
interesting in a male way.

The garden of Cabbot Hall was more enticing then
the house. Sarah wondered whether it had been thus
when the Mostyn Hallams bought it, or whether it was
here that Winifred Hallam exercised her imagination. It
was a random garden, full of rough patches, chance flow-
ers or shrubs in unpredictable places, rich corners where
you had expected nothing. She enjoyed her ramble, and
she only turned back towards the house because she was
uncertain how long "drinks" were supposed to last. It
was as she was going through a well-stocked kitchen garden, at the corner of the house, that she was unexpectedly
addressed.

"Good evening, young lady. You must be the new
acquisition in the neighbourhood."

Sarah jumped. She was nervous anyway, being in a
strange environment, and among strangers. But there was
something about the voice too . . . It was soft, slightly
sibilant, but with reserves of power and harshness, as if
the man could very easily play the bully. With the insight
that seemed to have taken charge of her that day, Sarah
said:

"Major Coffey?"

The man's smile was crooked, yet complacent.

"I have been pointed out to you."

He had not, but Sarah did not correct him. Perhaps her moment of insight had not been so surprising. The man's back had a parade-ground straightness that made him stand out among all these gentlemen-farmers and tradespeople. He was tall, thin, his face sunken and sallow, with a military moustache and bright, piercing eyes. He looked very fit for his age, which must have been over fifty, but at the same time he impressed Sarah vividly as a very uncomfortable man—not in himself, but for others. He had been standing in shadow, under an apple tree. Was he shunned by the other guests? Had he been waiting for her? Already Sarah wanted very much to get away.

"And you are the new nursemaid at Hallam."

"Yes," said Sarah shortly. She did not elaborate on Chloe's being at the stage of emerging from the nursery.

"A remarkable family you have come into. Clan, I almost called them. They keep very close. Very close indeed."

He made it sound very unpleasant. Sarah immediately felt defensive.

"I don't think Mr. Dennis and Mr. Mostyn Hallam are particularly close."

"Not politically. I am talking about as a family." He looked down at her confidingly, as if he were sharing a secret. "Did you know both gentlemen married cousins? No? That's what I mean by being clannish. It's not wise, you know. Not good for the racial stock. It will not have escaped your notice that our host is childless."

This was too silly for Sarah to let pass.

"Whereas the Dennis Hallams have four children," she pointed out. "You can prove anything if you choose the right example."

"Ah—a quick-witted young lady! Exactly what I would have expected from someone employed at Hallam. Something of an intellectual hot-house, that establishment, you will find."

"The Hallams are intelligent people," retorted Sarah. "That is a pleasanter way of putting it."

"Ah, you think I am being unpleasant about your employers? Well, there's no denying we have a very different attitude to things. You see, to me they *are* essentially sterile—in their pathetic pacifism, for example. It's very un-English, you know. It doesn't go down at all well with the gentry around here, nor with the village people either. Fortunately the English countryside still produces a very sturdy, patriotic type of lad."

"I believe I know the English countryside and its people quite as well as you do, Major," said Sarah. "Tell me, did you stop me just now simply to malign my employers?"

"Malign?" he said, his voice soft and insinuating, his smile crooked. "Not at all, young lady. I am merely trying to make you more aware of the Hallams and their position here. They are very attractive, persuasive people. No doubt you have found them so, am I not right? That makes it so easy for them to infect—is that too strong a word?—"

"Yes."

"I think not. Infect other people with their own craven, defeatist notions. I believe that people exposed to them should be on their guard—particularly a *young* person, and a young *lady*—"

"Major Coffey, I am not feeble-minded."

"By no means," he said, with a sketch of a bow. "You have a strength of mind I admire. I try to gather around me young people with spirit, with pride and patriotism. It would give me great pleasure to introduce you—"

"I'll not trouble you to make my friends for me," said Sarah, her blood boiling, walking away quickly.

"Remember," the voice hissed behind her, "the Hallams' notions are not liked. The people here are not lily-livered intellectuals. They may find ways of showing their feelings!"

3

The next two weeks were a time of joy and discovery for Sarah. The only troubled moments were the comings and goings of Will, and the obvious anxiety of his parents.

As the Republican government of Spain began to fight back, young radicals all over Britain began to organize themselves to go to their aid. That much, at any rate, was clear from Will's conversation. But he was careful to confine himself to generalities—names were not mentioned, nor specific projects or plans. He was obviously afraid that his parents would make attempts to stop him if they knew what his intentions were, and who else was involved in them.

"But I don't see how we *can* stop him," said Helen tearfully to Sarah. "We've always let our children make their own decisions, and he's quite right that in all essentials he is of age. But if only he would *think* . . ."

But Will's mind was on action rather than on meditation.

"This is going to be the testing-ground," he declared one evening, when he had arrived home on a flying visit. "If all the anti-Fascist forces can get together, get them-

selves organized and fighting-ready, then we'll be an un-
beatable force. We'll turn the tide. If we fail here, we'll
fail everywhere."

Dennis Hallam said nothing. In truth his efforts to
organize international and non-violent opposition to the
revolt were not having much success. It looked as though
what Will had said about the people in government having only sympathy for the Spanish generals was proving
to be nothing but the truth. In his heart Dennis had
known that from the start. His fair, handsome face bore
much of the time lines of worry, or near-despair.

It was a little over two weeks after the revolt had
broken out that Will paid a visit home that lasted all of
two days. Sarah and all the family were conscious that a
great deal of sorting and packing was taking place in his
room. Large cartons of stuff were put out for the dust-
man, which had an unmistakable implication that the
Hallam part of his life was over. He was thoughtful for
much of the time at meals, but then made slightly forced
attempts to behave normally—playing Snap with Chloe
and backgammon with his father, doing both with boisterous high spirits that did not entirely ring true.

When he went to bed on the second night, he stood
up and said, with boyish awkwardness:

"I'm catching the early train tomorrow, so I'll say
good night."

And he went up and kissed his mother and Elizabeth,
and almost shook hands with his father and brother—
then, apparently finding this smacked of the ridiculous,
he darted from the room. Nobody was in any doubt what
this meant.

"I'm not going to cry," Helen Hallam said. "I do feel
this means that somehow we've failed Will, but being
against war doesn't mean you can't salute bravery, and I

think Will is very brave. Please God he comes back safely."

She didn't cry, but Sarah was sure that when, soon after, she too went to her bed, it was to do just that.

The house without Will, and without the prospect of Will returning, was a sadder and a quieter place. He had had a vitality and a force that none of the others had: he had lighted up the place, which now appeared dim, under lit. Sarah found her days centering on Chloe, which was natural. Her job, as Mrs. Hallam had explained when she had first been interviewed, was to bring Chloe out of the nursery and give her first lessons. Chloe, though, was far from in the state of nature that one would have expected in a child of a more normal family of gentry. In fact, Sarah found that, as was natural in a household which revolved around books, Chloe had scraped a bit of tuition here, and a bit there, and could already read quite capably. Her writing fist was uncertain, resembling nothing so much as a punch-drunk boxer's, still wearing gloves. But she was a naturally delicate child, and in a matter of days Sarah was registering an improvement. It was to be her task, she thought, to forward the education process without dampening the natural joyousness of this exotically beautiful young animal.

How long she was to have charge of her Sarah did not know. "Certainly a year, possibly two, maybe even more," Helen Hallam had said at the interview. Where she was to go to school was as yet unclear. The Hallams appeared unusually uncertain on the subject of education. Oliver had gone to his father's old school, Wellington, but Will and Elizabeth had gone to day schools near Banbury, and this, Sarah gathered, was not from any financial considerations. It probably would turn out that Chloe would attend some similar sort of place, but meanwhile Sarah had the pleasure of supervising the first stages of her education. It seemed likely to prove a stimulating and pleasurable experience.

"We wanted somebody *young,*" Helen said to her. "You can't expect the other children to have much time for her, and the child of older parents can become so *quaint,* if one's not careful. Mrs. Munday has been the principal person in her life so far, and of course she's a dear, but she's even older than Dennis and me, so we want you gradually to take her place."

Sarah did not see her job as being confined to the schoolroom, though a little room that had served for the older children was made available, and there were children's books and school books galore around the house, many of which Chloe already knew. Sarah often took the child around the grounds of Hallam, teaching her about trees and birds and trying to arouse in her the first glimmerings of her own passion for the natural world. Any knowledge the child had picked up had been at random, gleaned from the conversation of adults.

Soon they went further afield, around the country lanes, and into the nearby villages. Here Chloe felt very much at home, and could draw on a great store of information.

"That's Mrs. Wicklow, and she's got a parrot that's fifty years old. She bought it from a sailor in Golden Jubilee year, and it has a terrible vo-vocab-ulary . . . That's the Rectory, but the Rector's very ill, and they'd like the Bishop to appoint a new one . . . That's Mrs. Fallow's Jim, who's a bit wild, and she's afraid he'll go away for a soldier, and she won't have any prop for her old age."

"Is he an only child, then?"

"Yes. Mrs. Fallow hates the army because she had two brothers who were killed in the Big War."

"We usually call it the Great War, Chloe."

"Great War . . . And that's Mrs. Widdicomb, who we get our eggs from. She has chickens in the back garden, and one of them is the best layer in all Oxfordshire . . . That cottage is Major Coffey's. He's a Fash . . . Fash . . ."

"Fascist."

"Fascist, and we don't talk to him if we can help it, though we are perfectly polite to him if we have to."

Most of Chloe's knowledge of the villages, Sarah realized, came from Mrs. Munday, as did many of the old-fashioned phrases she used to describe people. The nearest village to Hallam was Chowton, but it formed part of a trio of small communities, the others being Hatherton and Willbury. They were close enough to each other to be able to share some amenities, the Senior School being in Chowton, the village hall in Willbury, the doctor at Hatherton. The best butcher was in Willbury, and the best greengrocer in Chowton. Chowton was also the prettiest, but they all had their charm, and occasionally in summer little knots of undergraduates came out, often in hikers' gear, and stopped for beer and bread and cheese at one of the pubs. The local inhabitants favoured the bicycle as a form of transport, though the horse had not been entirely superseded, and small cars were eyed enviously.

"That's Mr. Cobham's Morris Minor," Chloe would announce. "He cleans it every Saturday morning, rain or shine. He bought it when his mother died, with the money she had stuffed in the sofa cushions in her best parlour."

So the walks became an enjoyable two-way process of communication and education.

"That's Roland," said Chloe, pointing to a young back. Its owner was looking into the window of a toys and games and stationery and all-sorts-of-things shop—the sort of shop Sarah knew rather well from Derbyshire.

"Who's Roland?"

"He's *nice.*"

Her confident definition, loudly delivered, had him swinging round. Sarah realized at once that she had, somewhere, seen him before. Of course—the young waiter at Mostyn Hallam's "drinks."

"Somebody must be talking about me," he said.

"I only said you were nice," said Chloe, loud and charming in self-justification. "What are you doing?"

"Looking to see what I can buy my little brother for his birthday next week."

"How old is he?" asked Sarah.

"Seven. I can't remember what I liked when I was seven."

"Perhaps Chloe could help."

"I'm sure Chloe has very expensive tastes. She looks a costly young woman. She'd choose something that was way outside the range of things I could afford."

"No I shouldn't. I know *all* about money, and I manage my own *very* well."

"Well, you go in and find out what you think he'd like, and how much it costs, and then come out and tell me, and I'll decide whether I can afford it or not. That way I won't be embarrassed by having to put it back."

Chloe smiled with a satisfied sense of her own importance, and went into the shop. They watched her climb the steps and reach up to the latch, smiling. Roland turned his square, humorous, countryman's face to look directly into Sarah's.

"I sent her in so we could get to know each other."

"I know."

"Well, it's not often we see new faces in these villages. I thought I'd go through the whole of the summer without seeing anyone I didn't know already."

"What happens at the end of summer?"

"I go back to Oxford. I'm at Oriel, on a scholarship. It enables me to live and eat, but not much more. The summer vac lasts very long indeed."

"Oh, I see. Hence the job waiting up at Cabbot Hall."

"That's right. But unfortunately that sort of job is few and far between. Of course what I'd like is to get a regular job for two or three months, but what chance is there of that, with millions unemployed? Mr. Hallam—Mostyn Hallam—has been very good to me. He helped me with the scholarship application, and gave me a reference. There've been one or two jobs like the one you saw me doing, which help me to get by . . . I was rather glad Oliver Hallam wasn't there, though."

"Why?"

"We're on the League of Nations Union committee together. Silly, isn't it, not to want to be seen serving drinks? He knows perfectly well how I'm situated financially, yet I didn't want him to see me . . . I'm ashamed of myself, but . . ."

"You must be one of the few young men in the villages around here to have gone to Oxford. Here it all seems . . . Oxfordshire, but not Oxford, so to speak."

"That's right. I'm the only one."

"Major Coffey was going on to me at the party about the sturdy type of village lad around here."

Roland twisted his mouth down in an expression of wry disgust, then laughed frankly.

"That sounds like our local Blimp. I went to one or two of his gatherings years ago. I'm sturdy enough, but I don't think it's the right kind of sturdiness."

"Is he as nasty as he seems?"

Roland considered. He seemed to dislike snap judgements.

"Maybe. Or, looking at him another way, you could call him pathetic. He lives on myths and forgotten ideals. And he tries to order reality to fit in with his fantasies."

"But is he a Fascist?"

"I suppose so. Maybe that's what Fascists do: try to make their myths concrete. He had a small but flourishing group in London after the war: the British Empire Union. Patriotism and racial purity and all that stuff. When Mosley formed his movement, Coffey was dished, and he moved to the country. What's happened has been that he's just formed a local chapter of his old party here. At least he's much less dangerous—*even* less dangerous —in Oxfordshire."

"You obviously don't think he is dangerous."

"Not really. For example, I know lots of men around here of my age, and some of them went to his group for years. Then they grew out of it, and now they laugh about him over a pint in the Silent Swan. They're adults, and they see it was silly."

"Is he—" Sarah hesitated. This was not something ever talked about in her vicarage, and she flushed even as she tried to phrase the question. "Is he . . . unnatural?"

"Homosexual? I suppose so. But largely unconscious, I would guess. His whole life has been spent among men, remember. There's a strong vein of cruelty there: he commanded a unit of the Black and Tans in Dublin after the

war, and he talks of firing squads in France executing
'cowards' . . . Of course, you're right: he is very nasty.
But I don't think one should make the mistake of taking
him too seriously."

Chloe emerged from the shop.

"I think what you should buy him," she announced,
looking up into Roland's face, "is a lovely pack of Happy
Families. They're all coloured in lots of colours, and Mrs.
Bunn the Baker's Wife is the nicest I've ever seen. And
it's only a shilling."

"Good. That sounds like a sensible selection. I'll go in
and buy it." Roland turned to Sarah. "I say, they have
films twice a week at the village hall in Willbury. They
have talkies even. You wouldn't like to come some time,
would you?"

"Oh, *do* go," said Chloe, dancing up and down. "It's
lovely. It keeps breaking down, and everybody talks
about what should happen next, and sometimes they take
bets. It's much better than sitting through a whole film
without a break. And you can get ice-cream, because Mr.
Cubbins next door opens his shop when the interval is
coming."

"It sounds irresistible," said Sarah. "I'd love to go. I
must see when I can get off."

"You do get time free?"

"Yes, I'm sure I do. But we have a guest coming to
Hallam tonight. A friend of Oliver's from Oxford—an
Indian student."

Roland laughed.

"That'll give ammunition to Major Coffey. But practically anything your Hallams do does that. It shouldn't
stop you getting away for the evening, should it?"

"I don't think so. I'll telephone you—"

She stopped, flushing. Of course he was unlikely to have a telephone.

"You can ring Matchett the Baker. He's next door, and my mother works for him sometimes. Mind you do."

They said their goodbyes, and Roland watched them until they were well down the High Street on their way back to Hallam. Then he went into the shop and bought his brother a small cricket bat. It was a long time before Chloe found out, not till she was a grown up woman, but she called him "Faithless Roly" for the rest of his life, and said he was born for diplomacy and the civil service.

Sarah went that evening with Dennis and Oliver to fetch Oliver's friend. Helen said she had a slight headache, but Sarah knew she was still upset about Will's departure. She also knew that when the guest arrived Helen would be the perfect hostess. The station was at Hatherton, and they took Bumps again. The train was late. Oliver said that the trains that stopped at Hatherton always were, except when you banked on their being so and arrived late to meet them. It was getting dark, for Oliver's guest had had to go to a meeting in London, one calling for immediate Indian independence, before taking the train for Oxford, and then catching the connection to Hatherton. Oliver spoke to the station master about his children as they waited, and Dennis and Sarah walked up and down the platform. Dennis wondered aloud—he could not keep off the subject—whether Will was still in Britain, and how soon the international volunteers would get involved in the real fighting.

It was a *very* local train, when it slowly drew up— rather dirty carriages, with no corridor. Oliver's friend was called Chan, which sounded Chinese rather than Indian to Sarah, and he was quiet, be-suited and friendly. Sarah had never met an Indian before, and was somewhat in awe. He spoke a beautiful, precisely articulated English, and when she got used to his misuse of the continuous present tense she had no difficulty in following what he was saying.

At first he did not say much at all, but when Dennis asked him about the meeting, he became more voluble.

"The government is not listening to what we are saying, Mr. Hallam. That old Baldwin, he is not interesting himself in the question of India. So the question we are asking ourselves is: how are we to make him listen?"

"Passive disobedience, you mean?"

"That is what we are discussing. But among other things, because we have many other options, and there are many who are arguing for something stronger."

There was something unreal for Sarah about driving through the narrow country roads of Oxfordshire in the gathering dark, and talking about ways of achieving independence for India. She resolved to have a good talk on the subject with Chan while he was there, but meanwhile she switched off. Dennis drove carefully and well, and Sarah thought about Roland, and when she would try to go with him to the picture show. As they drove through the gates of Hallam and up towards the house, Chan expressed his appreciation.

"A truly English house, just as we are always imagining them to be. It is a very fine specimen, is it not, of Tudor domestic architecture?"

"Rather good," said Dennis, bringing the car to a halt round the side of the house. He never put the Austin in its little garage by the stables during the summertime. They got out, and Dennis pointed out to Chan the fine chimneys, the beautiful proportions, the warmth of the brick. The two of them led the way round to the front of the house.

"My wife will have something ready for your supper," he said, as they approached the front door. "She's greatly looking forward to meeting—"

Dennis stopped in his tracks. Chan stopped too, and was forced to look where Dennis was looking, at the front door. Strapped against the heavy Tudor oak, hanging over the brass door-knocker, was what looked like a stuffed dog. It was a yellow-coloured, mongrelish dog, and it was secured in a cradle of white webbing. Dennis, going up to the door, realized with a jolt that was physical, and visible to Chan, that it was not a stuffed one, but a recently dead one, its face twisted as if in pain. On one band of the webbing, crudely lettered in indelible ink, he read the words:

yeLLow cuR

Looking down, he saw that, congealing on the steps, there lay a pool of blood.

Dennis, leaning against the doorpost, retched and retched, as if he had swallowed some terrible poison.

4

The main thing, everybody agreed, was not to let Chan's visit be spoiled. Some atavistic instinct about hospitality meant that, right from the first, the Hallams and their dependents tried to put the incident behind them. When they got inside Helen was told about it in a whisper by Oliver, and she suggested to him that he remove the beast at once to the garage, until they had decided what to do about it. Then she and Elizabeth took Chan off to the kitchen to meet Mrs. Munday and Pinner, and then they got him to bring in the food for the little supper that had been prepared—a move that effectively removed any sense of awkward superfluousness that Chan might have felt.

Sarah, alone in the sitting-room with Dennis, went over to the sideboard and poured him a glass of brandy. Why brandy, rather than whisky, gin, vodka, curaçao, or any of the other bottles that the sideboard carried in such lavish and useful profusion Sarah did not know. It was just that brandy was the drink always mentioned at the vicarage in connection with shocks, accidents or upset stomachs. It certainly seemed to do the trick in this case. In a couple of minutes colour had flooded back into Den-

nis's cheeks, and he was smiling at Sarah in self-deprecation.

"I've really no right to go queasy at the sight of
blood," he said, shaking his head. "When you think how
much those poor beggars on the Western Front saw, I'm
ashamed. We had little enough of it in Egypt and the
Near East. It's some sort of instinctive revulsion, but
luckily it passes quite quickly. Let's make sure the rest of
the evening is pleasant for Chan."

And pleasant it certainly was, in a quite unforced
way. Chan ate with a will, and Mrs. Munday had prepared a delightfully dainty and English light meal. Elizabeth played the piano for a while, and her mother sang a
couple of Schubert songs. Oliver promised to show Chan
the house next morning and Dennis talked over with him
the book he was currently reviewing, about Britain's role
in nineteenth-century Afghanistan. Only Bounce, whin-
ing and shifting his position with great sighs, showed he
was uneasy. All in all it was a happy couple of hours, and
though Sarah was sure that Chan was likely to remember
the grotesque spectacle of the dead dog before he went to
sleep, still, that memory should at least be overlaid by
something less hideous.

It had been decided by breakfast-time that they would
have to tell the police. For a start Oliver said he suspected
that the dog had been deliberately and not accidentally
killed. Then Sarah, hesitantly, told them about Major
Coffey's veiled threats. Mrs. Munday said that if it was a
yellowy-looking creetur, it was probably Mrs. Battley's.
Helen was adamant: they couldn't have people saying
that they were responsible for the death of a widow's dog.

"It was probably her only companion," she said.
"We'll simply have to have somebody looking into it,

even if nothing comes of it. Oh, and Sarah—*please* keep Chloe away from the garage until it's gone."

So while Oliver gave Chan a conducted tour of the house, and while Sarah tried to keep Chloe's mind on her story book in the schoolroom, Dennis and Helen Hallam talked about the nasty incident of the night before with Sergeant South.

"The police" in that trio of Oxfordshire villages, and in the fields and woods beyond, meant Sergeant South. He was a tall, well-built countryman, one who had been in his time a "fine figure of a man," and the sort of policeman whose proximity gives confidence to timid old ladies and shy children, and gives others pause to think. Now he was a few years beyond his physical prime, and beer and sausages and hearty breakfasts had led to that heavy belt being let out a notch or two. But he was still impressive, still a presence, and though he was slow, he was not stupid. It was a distinction that Helen Hallam seemed ready to make, but Dennis Hallam had to mask his impatience at the ponderousness with which the interview was conducted.

"I have had a look at the animal," said Sergeant South, after he had led Dennis through a recital of the discovery of the beast hanging on his front door. "There's little doubt in my mind that there is Liz Battley's Rover."

There was nothing, almost, that Sergeant South did not know about the surface life of the villages that were under his surveillance. Some of the undercurrents, it is true, were unknown to him, and inconceivable to his type of mind, but he had a brilliant grasp of facts and relationships.

"Liz Battley?" Dennis Hallam furrowed his handsome brow. "Let me see, isn't she widow of one of our workers on Matcham Farm? Has one of the cottages on the outskirts of Chowton, doesn't she? On the road to Hatherton?"

"That's right, sir."

"Her husband had a heart attack, round about harvest time one year," put in Helen.

"He did. She's been a widow lady these eight, nine years . . . Never had cause to quarrel with her, sir, madam, have you? She couldn't have any sort of grievance against you?"

"Of course not, Sergeant. I'm sure I would recognize her if I saw her in the street, but at the moment I can hardly put a face to her."

"She worked here once or twice to help out, and has always been quite friendly," said Helen quietly. "Of course she has no grudge against us. And you're not suggesting, Sergeant, that she'd kill her own pet . . . Oh, I suppose the dog *was* killed, wasn't it?"

The sergeant looked up, slowly and thoughtfully.

"I can only give you a layman's opinion, Mrs. Hallam. I'll have a vet look at it soon as possible. It's had its throat cut, poor beast, but I suppose it could have been done just after death—so that there would be some blood." Dennis looked away, briefly. "So I'd not rule out that it was hit by a motor-car first. But I'd say someone just cut his throat."

"Wouldn't that be difficult?" Dennis asked. "It seemed quite a big dog. Wasn't it fierce?"

"Not it, sir. Well, it could put up a show, like, but nobody as knowed it would be scared of it. It roamed the villages most of the time, and it was a bit of a daft animal: suddenly it'd decide to have a good bark at someone—just to let off steam, like. But it they held out their hand and said: 'Come on, Chink—good boy,' he'd go to them, waggin' his silly tail."

"Chink?"

"The village boys called him that. On account of him being so yellow," said Sergeant South, unembarrassed. "And if anyone made a fuss of him, he'd follow them for miles."

"So that's how he could have been brought here . . . a dog to the slaughter," said Helen, in a faint voice.

"Yes, he could. Well, now, sir, there's the question of this writing on that there webbing."

"Yes, I think we should talk about that."

Dennis's voice was very definite, but Sergeant South twisted his cap awkwardly.

"I don't know if you've any ideas about what they might mean, sir?"

"Of course," said Dennis briskly. "They're an accusation of cowardice."

"It's an odd accusation against a man who fought and was wounded in the war."

"Oh—" Dennis gestured dismissively with his arm— "I hardly saw any action at all. The war is ancient history now, and this is a matter of today. It's a comment on my work for the League of Nations, my opposition to rearmament . . ."

"Would you call yourself a pacifist, sir?"

Dennis thought for a moment.

"I don't know if I'd *call* myself one, but I suppose the positions I—we—adopt come pretty close to pacifism."

"The question is: who in the village would bother about that, one way or the other."

Sergeant South had stopped taking notes, and he was sitting back in his chair, more relaxed.

"I think you know the answer to that, Sergeant," said Dennis.

"You'd be referring to Major Coffey, I take it sir . . .

Well, I'd not be wanting to jump to conclusions, but the name does spring to mind."

"He's been egging on the village boys to get up some nasty prank against me. He practically said as much to our new governess."

"As you say, sir. I've no evidence, but that thought had occurred to me too. The problem is, granted that that's what happened, how to pin it down any further."

"What do you mean?"

"I mean, the Major and these boys don't form any organization, in the usual sense. The lads just go to his cottage from time to time. Then the Major, if he's wise, won't have egged them on to do this, won't have organized the prank as you call it (I'd prefer a nastier word) himself. He'll have gone about it in a much more round-about way. 'Wouldn't it be amusing if—' Do you get my meaning, sir?"

"I do."

"And that way he's in the clear. And even if we could be quite sure which of the village lads had actually done it, it would be far from clear what we could charge him with."

Dennis thought. He was a magistrate, and he appreciated the difficulty.

"Yes, I take your point. What do you suggest?"

"The best thing to my mind, sir, would be for me to start asking round a bit, talking to the boys, finding a likely culprit—maybe two or three likely ones—and then putting the fear of God into them. That way I'll hope to prevent a repetition, and maybe weaken the hold Coffey has over them."

"I think that's a vain hope," said Dennis impatiently, and with a trace of bitterness in his voice. "Apparently he's a local hero. He hasn't exhausted his credit, as I

have. He has four years' service, not to mention his he-
roic action against the Irish."

"I think you're mistaken, sir. Major Coffey isn't any
hero to most people in the villages, other than to the
young lads who don't know any better."

"Will you talk to him?" asked Dennis wearily.

"I'll hope to, eventually, sir. But he's quite a different
proposition from the lads, a really slippery customer.
He'll have a much better idea of the limits of the law, and
what he can do within it. He has had this movement of
his in London, and now and then they went pretty far."

"And his time with the Black and Tans will have
given him a taste for independent action. Oh yes—Major
Coffey will have a very good idea of how far he can go."

"To a degree our hands are tied, you see. But I'll do
what I can, and I'd like to say I'm sorry you've had this
nasty experience, sir." Sergeant South got up. "Now
there's the matter of that dog, sir. I suppose it wouldn't
be possible for your man to drive him down to the station
for me, would it, sir?"

That was what happened. Pinner put two horse blan-
kets over the back seat of the Austin Seven, and Mrs.
Battley's Rover, known to the village boys as Chink, was
driven to the council house which served as Sergeant
South's dwelling and doubled as a police station. Sarah
never felt quite the same about Bumps thereafter. A vet
was summoned from Banbury, the nearest town of any
size, and he pronounced that the dog had had its throat
cut, and had been hung on the door shortly afterwards.
One day, walking with Chloe in the grounds of Hallam,
Sarah came on a dry brown patch, which she discovered
was not brown grass, but something sticking to green
grass. It was by an overgrown bed about a hundred yards
from the house. Sarah mussed it about with her shoe, and

said nothing. There was no point in upsetting people by carrying the matter any further.

Because the whole family was now preoccupied with making Chan's stay a happy one, with erasing memories of its beginnings. They found he was rather good at tennis, and Oliver took him to tennis parties at neighbouring families. They chugged around the countryside visiting beauty spots, and they took the Wolseley into Oxford, to dinner at the Randolph and theatre afterwards. They had their political friends round for drinks, and the young Oxfordshire gentry round for tea on the lawn.

It was one day when Chloe was away at a birthday party (she had looked enchanting in her short, frilly frock, her hair shining and be-ribboned) that Sarah managed to have her walk and talk with Chan. They did talk about Indian independence, as Sarah had planned, but they also ranged over the world social and political scene, for Chan was very well-informed. Sarah was a good listener, and genuinely interested, and Chan was by now, after a week with the Hallams, a confident and fluent talker on topical matters. As they came to the village and people passed them in the streets they saluted Sarah, by now a familiar figure, and looked curiously at Chan. Sarah saw out of the corner of her eye that little triangles of curtain had been delicately raised, to afford the inhabitants of the cottages a glimpse of that most curious of phenomena, a dark-skinned man. Sarah was sure that Chan had not noticed, and was glad. They stopped and looked in shop windows, lingered outside the baker's to relish the smell, and they popped together into the newsagent's to fetch the Hallam copy of the *New Statesman and Nation,* and to purchase a bag of bullseyes. They were, Sarah informed her companion solemnly, a very British institution.

Many years later, in the 'sixties, when Chan was Mr.
Chandrakant Naran Desai and Deputy High Commis-
sioner for India in London, Sarah found herself sitting
beside him at a stuffy Whitehall dinner, and they laughed
as they remembered the bullseyes, and the way they had
walked through the village sucking them, while Chan
had read to Sarah what Kingsley Martin had to say about
the civil war in Spain.

"And all the village people looking at me and then
down at the ground, and the ones inside twitching their
curtains up to get a look," laughed Chan, by now a portly
figure, and one of great confidence and dignity. The other
diners, who were brought together by a trade mission
that seemed destined to achieve nothing whatsoever,
looked at the pair and wondered what anyone at such a
function could find to laugh at. Soon Chandrakant Desai
became serious.

"But you know, Sarah—may I still call you Sarah?
We are such old friends!—those two weeks at Hallam
were the happiest times I ever had in Britain. I look back
and I remember them as all sun, and teas on the lawn,
and happy games. They were—how do you say it?—hal-
cyon days for me, the most wonderful time of all my
student days."

"Yes," agreed Sarah, "the Hallams had the gift of
making people feel at home."

"Did they ever find out who killed that poor dog?"
asked Chan, and Sarah realized that he was quite unaware of all that had befallen the Hallams after his departure. How strange that events which had shaped her own
life, shadowed others, should have remained totally unknown to Chan.

The topic of the dog was to surface again, on that
walk the two of them took in August 1936. When they

got to the end of Chowton, they turned to walk back home. There was to be tea on the lawn again that day, with friends invited. But before they had gone more than a few steps, they were accosted by a gaunt woman in a shabby frock and apron, leaning over her cottage garden gate.

"Miss—Miss—I don't know your name, but you're up at the Hall, aren't you?"

"That's right. I'm Sarah Causeley."

The woman's manner was rough enough, in its country way, but underneath was an undertone of the desire to please, or perhaps of the old respect for the "quality." Sarah thought she had seen her once, doing cleaning work at Hallam.

"Will you be so kind, miss, as to say to Mrs. Hallam and Mr. how sorry I am that my owd dog was used to play that nasty trick on them. Give them a nasty turn, that would."

"Oh, you must be Mrs. Battley. I know Mrs. Hallam was *very* sorry about your dog. She knew how upset you would be. That's really disgusting, killing an animal like that."

"That's right. They didn't ought ter 'ave done that. 'Tworn't like as if it were a rabbit, or a stoat. He had no harm in him, that owd dog. But you tell Mrs. Hallam I'm right sorry."

In spite of her words Liz Battley seemed to have a stoical lack of indignation: the dog was dead, and that was it. Sarah had a sharp vision of village life in which death stood shoulder to shoulder with life in strange intimacy, in which stoats and rabbits were natural prey and their carcases had a grim familiarity. Suddenly she saw how the village lads had gone over the top into the mud of France and Flanders, to a death that was all but cer-

tain, with a dogged acceptance of the inevitable, without
thought of resistance or mutiny.

Both she and Chan were quieter on their way back.

When, heavy-footed, they came up to the house, they
saw that the company had arrived. The familiar tables
were set out on the lawn, and Pinner and Mrs. Munday
were going backwards and forwards, taking out crockery
and goodies. From the deckchairs talk and laughter
came, floating across the lawn to them. As she turned
and walked with Chan towards the assembled group,
Sarah felt no twinge of nervousness, no sense of strange-
ness, as she had so recently on her first day. She was part
of this scene, a member of this company. The vicarage in
Derbyshire seemed very far away. She was at home.

5

Towards the end of Chan's stay the Hallams had a postcard from Will. Sarah was reading a letter from home, in which her mother was worrying over some dizzy spells she had had recently, but she put it aside when Helen began reading Will's message. He was near Hendaye, where they were setting up a camp for refugees and wounded from Spain. There was a tremendous spirit among the Republican supporters, and if it was enthusiasm that counted, Will said, they couldn't lose. He would be going to Spain in a week or two's time, to join up with some foreign volunteers already there, with the pro-governmental forces. He sent his love to all of them—and he showed himself a typical Hallam by including Sarah by name.

They were quiet for a few minutes after this. Then, as if by mutual consent, they resumed their breakfast and their discussion of neutral topics.

Elizabeth was still agonizing over whether to "do the Season" next year. Fiona Macauley was putting pressure on her, and really she did think it might be rather fun.

"Of course, I know you'd rather I didn't do it," she said to her parents.

"There's no question of us preferring that you didn't," said Dennis. "Of course you must do as you want."

"Well, you'd rather I didn't want to do that sort of thing."

"Perhaps it's something you have to get out of your system," said Helen comfortably.

"I don't think Elizabeth realizes the appalling and unsuitable young men she will have to mix with," said Dennis.

"It's the unsuitable young men who are the main attraction," drawled Elizabeth.

The topic dissolved in laughter, but Dennis added:

"Actually you'll find that most of them are younger versions of Cousin Mostyn."

Men, one way or another, were on Sarah's mind too. She had ascertained that the picture shows at the Willbury Village Hall were on Thursdays and Saturdays, and she had begged Thursday evening off from Helen, should she need it. She looked into the telephone book and got the number of Matchett the baker, and was just about to ring him and leave a message for Roland when she realized that she did not know his surname. Chloe apparently just knew him as Roland, and beyond the fact that he lived next door to the baker's she knew embarrassingly little about him. Elizabeth would probably know, but Sarah shrank from the girlish confidences that might be expected from her if she asked. Oliver certainly knew, but to ask him was out of the question. Mrs. Munday always knew everything that was to be known about the characters and doings in the villages, though how she found out when she seemed to be on her feet and bustling around at Hallam from morn to night Sarah did not know. But she was a frightful gossip, and Sarah shrank from providing her with material for conjecture.

In the end she just picked up the phone and managed as best she could.

"Oh, I'm sorry to bother you, but I believe you're willing to take messages for next door . . . For Roland."

"Oh yes, miss. Mrs. Bradberry will be in later. Can I give it to her then?"

"Yes . . . Yes, I'm sure that will be all right. Could you say that Sarah says she can be free on Thursday evening?"

By the afternoon the whole thing had been arranged.

Before she had her night out, Sergeant South had paid another visit to the house, and had brought the Hallams up to date with his inquiries.

"I've got as far as I can go with the boys," he said, sitting rather gingerly on the chintz sofa in the sitting-room, which was in panelled oak and apparently taken over by books, which stretched up the walls and littered all the table-tops and most of the chairs. Sergeant South approved of the panelled oak, but he didn't see how even a literary gentleman like Dennis Hallam could possibly have read all those books. "Short of actually finding the culprit, which I don't think at the moment I'm going to do, I've done all I can. Luckily there's a number of young men, as we said, who've been subject to the Major's influence and have come out—what's the word I want?—"

"Unscathed?"

"That's it. Or rather like going down with the measles and coming through, and never likely to have it again. To these chaps the Major's something of a figure of fun. On the other hand, there's a sort of clannishness . . ."

"We know, we know," said Dennis.

"And that means that those who've gone through that stage don't feel inclined to split on those lads who are still going through it. Still, I'm pretty sure I know the leaders in the Major's little pack now, and I'll be keeping an eye on them."

"Who are they?"

The sergeant hesitated.

"Well, I'd say Christopher Keene, Bertie Marsh and Jim Fallow. It's them I've had a word with. Separately. Told them they're being watched, and that the moment they step out of line I'll be down on them like a ton of bricks."

"Why?" Dennis's voice was tired, disappointed. "Why do you think they should do this to us?"

Sergeant South seemed puzzled how to reply. He was not always good on the whys of village life.

"They're three very different boys," he said hesitantly. "So I think there's a different answer in each case. A bit of fun in the one instance. Under influence in the second. Rebelliousness in the third."

"And do you think your 'word' with them will do any good?" asked Helen.

"I don't know," admitted South. "Ten years, five years ago, it would've, no question. Somehow there's not the same respect any longer. The villages have gone the way of the towns. There's a new spirit, a spark—which is not all bad—"

"No, no," put in Dennis.

"—but still it means I can't rely on my telling-off having the effect it once had. We'll hope that, combined with the feeling that I've got my eye on them, it will make them watch their step." He stood up. "You can be sure I'll keep it very much in mind—and the whole situation with the Major."

"You haven't spoken to him?" Dennis asked, following him to the door.

"No. I'm going to, that's for sure. But I want an occasion when I've got him at a bit of a disadvantage, when I've got something on him that I can bring up, if necessary. I want to catch him on the hop."

"That sounds very sensible."

Sarah, who was crossing the landing from her bedroom to the schoolroom, saw what happened next through the deep oaken well of the staircase. On the table by the sitting-room door Pinner had put a silver tray with the mid-morning post on it. Absently, still paying farewell courtesies to Sergeant South, Dennis picked up a light blue envelope. It seemed to be of a somewhat superior brand—inside it was lined with dark blue paper, on which had been stuck a large white feather which stood out against the sombre background. Dennis gazed at it for a second or two.

"Too absurd," he said, handing it to Sergeant South. "But I suppose it means the campaign goes on."

South took the envelope gingerly by its edges. Silently, almost sheepishly, he went through the door, and got on the bicycle which he had left against the wall of the house.

The whole business, Sarah decided, as she went through her day, was silly rather than anything more menacing. The Hallams had said nothing to other household members about the feather, and they were right to say nothing. Of course they had had to call in Sergeant South about the dead dog, so Dennis had had to show him this new manifestation. But as far as the others were concerned it was better to meet these lesser persecutions with a dignified silence. Whoever it was would soon get tired and go on to find their amusement elsewhere. She didn't intend to let it interfere with her enjoyment of the cinema show.

Which, Mrs. Munday informed her with the relish of a connoisseur, would be a great treat. It was *Grand Hotel* with Greta Garbo, Joan Crawford, and a host of lesser stars. It was by now three or four years old, but excitement in the villages was none the less intense. Mrs. Munday herself would be going to the Saturday showing, with her sister, and they intended buying a box of chocolates to make the occasion complete. Chocolates, Sarah gathered, were a treat that both Garbo and Crawford warranted, even separately. They would not have been indulged in for, say, "that Bette Davis," or Katharine Hepburn.

Roland and Sarah had arranged to meet at the crossroads in Chowton, and walk the two and a half miles to Willbury. They would not be the only ones doing so, not by a long chalk, Roland had said over the phone. So when they met by the signpost they were in a small way part of a village celebration, though they were also conscious of being watched. It gave Sarah quiet satisfaction that she was wearing the summer frock that was the nearest approach to prettiness in her whole wardrobe. She thought Roland looked rather handsome too, and unmistakably intelligent. His sports jacket and flannels sat well on his tough frame. They dawdled a little on the way there, because Roland was a friend of the projectionist (who was the son of the Willbury garage owner), and he was going to save them two good seats. Nobody quarrelled with the prerogatives of the projectionist. Sarah and Roland talked about the villages, about their plans for the future, and the political scene. Would Mr. Baldwin retire soon, and would it make any difference if he did? Sarah deliberately said nothing about the Hallams and the spate of persecution they were being subjected to.

The atmosphere in the Willbury Village Hall was warm—indeed it was more than an atmosphere, closer to a smell: it seemed compounded of well-worn clothes, sweat, potato crisps, with a distinct tang of the stable. It was a smell Sarah recognized from her Derbyshire upbringing. The audience shouted to each other, exchanged news and banter, and above all expressed anticipation for the evening's entertainment. It was an anticipation Sarah shared, without condescension or detachment: she had seen Garbo only twice before, and never in a speaking part, and she had heard that Joan Crawford was a very powerful actress. They took their seats feeling rather like royalty at a gala.

The warm-up film was a Laurel and Hardy. Performers and audience were made for each other, and the hall rocked with an uncomplicated laughter. It was quite short, because *Grand Hotel* was longer than usual. There was a break between films, but Roland said they shouldn't go out.

"We'll get an ice-cream when it breaks down."

"But it may not break down tonight."

Roland winked at her and smiled. Of course it would break down, Sarah realized. It would because the audience preferred it to break down—liked to stretch their legs, discuss performances, speculate on the story line. And of course when it did the sweet shop and general store next door would find itself open, and do a good trade keeping the audience fed and happy for the second half. Sarah should have realized. She knew village life.

When it did break down, about half an hour into the film, when all the various characters and plot-strands converging on the Grand Hotel had been presented and

intertwined, Sarah and Roland got up with a feeling of
satisfaction and went out into the twilight along with the
rest, or most of them—for some few of the very poorest
stayed in their seats, their meagre resources having run
out with the price of the ticket. The fresh air was nice,
and Sarah had an ice-cream, and Roland had a cup of
strange coffee—gritty, percolated with milk—which he
said he liked. Everyone was very jolly, and very involved
with the story. Sarah had realized during the first part of
the film that she had read a few chapters of the book
three or four years before, but that it had been called in
by the local library, to be sent down an impatient waiting
list. So she could join the rest in uninhibited speculation
about motives and mysteries, involvements and fates.

"See you got a new girl, Roly."

The voice was overloud, and Sarah turned, not best
pleased. The speaker was a teenage boy. His thin body
was clad in rather dirty work trousers and pullover, and
his head was too big for it. The expression on his face
seemed to combine vacancy with cunning. He was of the
village type that was usually said to be "not all there,"
though that expression of cunning and—what was it?—
relish made Sarah think that appearances might be de-
ceptive.

"That's right, Barry," said Roland—calm, kindly.

"You be the new girl up at the big house, that right?"
Barry asked, turning those large, distant eyes on Sarah.
The least she could do, she felt, was be as kind as Roland.

"Yes. I look after the little girl, Chloe."

"That right? . . . She be a pretty little thing, that
one . . ." Barry thought, and then he fixed Sarah with a
look that she found unnerving because the distant expression had now gone, and been replaced by a concentrated
expression of enjoyment, of that relish she had noted. He

said with a horrible chuckle: "I hear old man Hallam
can't stand the sight o' blood, that right?"

"Here, what do you mean—'old man Hallam'?" said
a woman's voice, from the back of the little knot of audience members. Sarah was glad of the intervention, because she had not been sure what to say. "You keep a
civil tongue in your head, Barry, when you're speaking to
the young lady."

"That right, though?" persisted Barry.

"There's a lot of people can't stand the sight of
blood," said Sarah carefully. "It's very common."

"Wouldn't be no good on a farm, though, would he?
Wouldn't be able to shoot no rabbits. Not if he goes sick
at the sight of a dead dog."

"That's enough o' that," said the woman's voice, and
Sarah recognized Liz Battley, who now came up and put
herself between them. "I don't want to hear no more
about my owd dog, and I don't want to hear no more
spite agin the Hallams." She lowered her voice. "He
don't mean no harm, miss, but he's only ten shillings in
the pound, and he's got no respect at all."

Sarah smiled her thanks, and nodded. She said she
hoped Mrs. Battley had got a new dog, and Mrs. Battley
said she'd wait and see what bitches produced. A bell
rang inside the hall, and Roland took her arm to lead her
back.

Behind her she could hear that overloud voice, with
its note of gloating, saying: "He do throw up, just for a
bit of blood."

"What's his name?" whispered Sarah.

"Barry Noaks," said Roland, in a low, troubled voice.
"I don't think there's any harm in the lad."

Sarah kept a tactful silence.

When the film resumed she forgot about the incident,

and immersed herself in the tangled drama. Films were
still a treat and a novelty to her, and she had no difficulty
involving herself on a surface level. Decades later, as an
old woman, she saw the film on afternoon television, and
the suffocating smell of the Willbury Village Hall came
back to her. She thought then how like the film was to
the soap operas to which she was devoted, and on which
she meditated an article for *New Society*. At the time she
saw it first there was no such thing as soap opera. She
murmured to Roland: "It's rather like *South Riding*—all
these different plots going in and out of each other." But
South Riding was still quite new—Sarah had pounced on
the copy at Hallam—and Roland hadn't read it.

And then suddenly, when all the rest of the audience
were silent, hushed by some moment of drama or pathos
on the screen, something in Sarah's mind posed the question: "How did he know?"

How did Barry Noaks know that Dennis had retched
helplessly at the sight of the dog's blood? She had told
nobody. Chan certainly would not have told anybody,
because he had less than no contact with the villagers. It
wasn't something Oliver would have gossiped about, and
she doubted whether the Hallams had even mentioned
the fact to Sergeant South. Dennis had brought nothing
up, so there had been nothing for Pinner or Mrs. Munday
to clean up.

The inference was obvious. Somebody had been
watching. Barry possibly, or more likely the boy who had
hung the dog on the door. Perhaps they were one and the
same person. She could see Barry slaughtering the dog,
but she couldn't imagine him as a member of Major Coffey's circle. The Major was interested in an altogether
smarter sort of boy—and perhaps, she wondered, blushing, in a very much better-looking sort too?

But *somebody* had been watching, and had talked. By now that silly, insignificant fact was all round the village.

It unsettled her for the rest of the film show. If she had been asked how the film ended, she wouldn't have been able to tell. She came to consciousness as the music swelled and somebody put the lights on.

"That was lovely," she said to Roland. He grinned.

"Marvellous tosh," he said.

On the way home they talked about the film, and about the villagers' reactions to it. "So direct," said Roland. "You'd never get anything so warm and spontaneous at Oxford." Sarah was hesitant about bringing up what was really in her mind. Roland was somebody whom she trusted, but really hardly knew. Also, she had no wish to make an issue or a talking point out of such a silly little matter. Her instinct was to let it die. However, eventually, as they were approaching Hallam, she said:

"I wonder how Barry knew about Mr. Hallam being sick."

Roland shrugged.

"It's common talk around the village. Only someone like Barry would make an issue of it. Most of the people with all their wits about them realize that Mr. Hallam is a bookish sort of man. They expect that type to be sensitive."

"I just wonder how they *know*. There were just the four of us in the car."

"I expect Mrs. Munday talked. She's a great gossip, you know, with the women who go up to Hallam to clean."

Sarah let it go at that. They said goodbye at the gate, very warmly, and Sarah promised to try to get another evening off soon. They did not kiss good night. Sarah never kissed her boyfriends (there had been two) on the first evening out. She believed only very fast girls did.

"Will you be all right up to the house?" asked Roland.

"Of course. It's only a couple of hundred yards. There's still some lights on, so there's still family up. I've got a key, anyway."

"I'll wait here till you're safely in."

That did give Sarah a feeling of extra security. She turned when she got to the door and waved. Once inside, she knocked on the door to the sitting-room and went in. It was Helen and Dennis who were still up, unusually late for them. Helen got up and went over to her.

"Sarah dear, there's a telegram arrived for you. From Derbyshire."

Helen knew, and Sarah knew, that telegrams did not arrive from home without there being bad news inside them. When she took the little brown envelope her hands were trembling, but she tore it open.

The message read baldly: MOTHER DIED THIS MORNING.

Sarah turned to Helen and sobbed on her breast, as she had never, since a little child, sobbed on the breast of the dead woman.

6

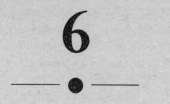

Oliver drove Sarah to the station next morning. They were both very quiet, but as they drew up at the ugly little building, Oliver said rather awkwardly, but in a touchingly grown-up voice:

"Whatever you decide, Sarah, remember that you have a home here too."

Her father, when much later she arrived at the vicarage in Stetford, also said very little. As he kissed her he told her the time of the funeral next morning. Later in the evening, as they were sitting silent in the dark front room of the vicarage, he said: "It's very inconvenient her dying just now—." Sarah was convinced that he had intended to add: "just before harvest festival," but had thought better of it.

The funeral was conducted by a clergyman from a neighbouring parish. So that her father could hide his own lack of emotion, Sarah thought. Then she chided herself for a cheap jibe: her father felt his wife's death as deeply as he was capable of feeling anything of an emotional nature. A slight by the Bishop, however, would have hurt him more.

He sat throughout the service icy and remote, appar-

ently contemplating arctic vistas. After the sad spectacle
at the graveside he received attempts at comfort and
commiseration in the same tight-lipped manner with
which, at Christmastime, he was accustomed to receiving
compliments of the season.

Back at the vicarage some attempt had been made to
provide fare for the principal mourners. It seemed to
Sarah that such food and drink as there was had been
provided, unasked, by Mrs. Wilcox and Mrs. Spencer,
wives of church-wardens. Her father had played no part
in the provision of it, and played next to no part in the
dispensing of it. Nobody knew whether they were meant
to go back to the vicarage, and nobody who went could
decide how long they ought to stay. They ate to hide their
embarrassment, and escaped as soon as was decent.

The women of the church—who in fact kept the con-
gregation together, since the Reverend Causeley's ministry seemed to concern itself solely with forms, tithes, and
marks of respect that should be paid to him personally—
were a comfort to Sarah. Her mother had done all the
things a vicar's wife was expected to do, and had done
them as well as anybody of her shy, dispirited nature
could be expected to do them. A vicar's family did after
all occupy (and the Reverend Causeley was extremely
forward in asserting it) some position in rural society—
lower than the local gentry, certainly, but at least as high
as the doctor. The big house in the area was seldom occupied, since the gentleman of the house was busy retrieving the family's fortunes in the City of London. Indeed,
local rumour had it that he was not so much retrieving
the family's fortunes as quite simply making a lot of
money for himself—that he would gladly have got rid of
the house if he could have found anybody foolhardy or
vainglorious enough to have bought it. Thus a consider-

able burden had fallen on Sarah's mother, and the ladies of the parish were warm—perhaps over-warm—in their praise of her manner of carrying it.

When they had all gratefully ducked off, there seemed nothing to do, nothing to say. Sarah took herself off for a walk, on a hill path where she could be quite certain she would be alone. The late afternoon sunlight restored her spirits. When she got home her father was in his study, no doubt "writing a sermon"—one of those dry discourses, like the financial statement of a company chairman, which showed little sign of the literary pains that were apparently bestowed on them. Whatever he was doing, he would certainly be happier on his own. Sarah found a book—it was *Angel Pavement,* which her mother had had out from the library. She would have to take it back in the morning. Meanwhile it would help to take her mind off the clock ticking.

Her father emerged from the study as the time approached for his little bit of supper. Sarah asked if he would like anything, and he murmured that he thought he could just manage a piece or two of toasted cheese. Sarah made several slices, some for herself, and they sat around the fire eating them. There was no intimacy. They said nothing. Only when her father had finished, and he sat wiping his fingers, did he say:

"How much notice do you think the Hallams will expect you to give?"

Unconsciously she had been expecting that question in one form or another. Perhaps it was Oliver who had prepared her mind for it. She had not planned an answer, but it came without hesitation:

"I shall not be giving notice. I shall go back to work there."

There was a long pause.

"So you do not intend to come back here?"

"No."

She went back to her book. When she had finished a chapter she began to clear the supper things away. Later in the evening, when Sarah had washed up and made two cups of cocoa, her father said, his voice now having an undertone of whine:

"But what is to become of me?"

"I'll talk to Mrs. Wilcox in the morning. I'm sure there are many women in the village willing to do the cooking and cleaning. I'll find the most reliable."

"But that will cost money."

"Yes."

It did not help that, next morning, when she went to talk to Mrs. Wilcox, she was greeted with: "Well, we'll be seeing more of you in the future, Sarah."

Sarah had taken off her ridiculous grey hat and coat, and sat in Mrs. Wilcox's semi-detached's sitting-room.

"Actually I shall be staying at my job, Mrs. Wilcox. That's what I've come to see you about."

"Staying at your job? But we assumed you'd be coming back to look after your father."

"Did you?"

"Well, naturally . . ."

"Do you think that's natural? I'm not sure that I do."

"But you being a daughter, and an only child . . ."

"Being a daughter shouldn't make you a natural choice for being a martyr. I've always intended to make some sort of career for myself, and I don't see any reason to change my plans."

"Well, I *am* surprised. I never thought of you as one of those modern young ladies, Miss Sarah."

"Didn't you? Perhaps I've only just found it out myself."

"But what's going to happen to your father?"

They chewed over the subject, and went through the candidates for cook and daily help. They selected the widow of a cowman, who would keep the house spotless, and would cook the vicar a substantial midday meal. She was also, Mrs. Wilcox said, scrupulously honest—which meant, Sarah knew, that she would not take more than the few scraps from the kitchen that she would regard as her legitimate perks.

"But she's got her three sons," said Mrs. Wilcox. "I don't know as she'd want to go back to the vicarage in the evening and cook the vicar his supper."

"I don't see that a man is incapable of learning how to cook a bit of toasted cheese, or open a tin of baked beans and heat it up," said Sarah briskly. She got from Mrs. Wilcox the going rate for the job, and by evening she had it all arranged.

When she left next morning, just before midday, the new help was already at home in the kitchen, and a steamed meat pudding was on the stove. Sarah had packed the night before, and had dawdled through the morning till she could decently leave. Her father had retired to the study, where he was doubtless polishing the annual balance sheet. Sarah adjusted her only, and dreadful, hat in front of the hall mirror. Nothing was going to make it look anything but ridiculous. Then, her heart thumping, she tapped on the study door and put her head round.

"Goodbye, Father."

"Goodbye."

He did not look up, and purposely did not say her name.

So that was it. She shut the front door and walked, case in hand, through the little village. News had obviously spread that she would not be coming back to look after her father, and some of his women parishioners gave her looks of disapproval. News had obviously not got to the station master, however, because as he clipped her ticket, he said:

"Guess we'll be seeing you back here soon, miss."

"Yes—I may come back for Christmas," she said insouciantly.

Now the news would spread to male and beer-drinking spheres.

The journey back to Oxfordshire would be slow and circuitous. The train was a tiny local one, going to Crewe, and she had a compartment all to herself. As it pulled almost imperceptibly out of the station she felt a great lifting of the heart, and, following that, a great surge of gratitude to the Hallams that she had not sold herself into slavery. It was Oliver's words that had prepared her, it was the Hallams who—quite unintentionally—had given her the confidence, the courage and the vision to know that martyrdom within a loveless family was wrong.

As the train chugged through heart-stopping scenery, Sarah suddenly jumped up and threw her hat to the roof with a joyful shout. She was free. Life was opening up before her. Then she laughed and laughed with relief, and when she stopped she didn't feel ashamed at all.

7

Sarah was greeted with great and loving kindness by the Hallams when she returned. Since the subject had never come out into the open between them, none of them asked her if she had made any decision to stay or to return home. When she resumed her ordinary duties next day and said nothing that seemed to augur departure, the Hallams took her decision as read, and were obviously pleased. Eventually Helen Hallam asked her how she thought her father would cope, and what arrangements she had made for him. When they had discussed it for a little—Sarah displaying that reticence that spoke volumes —Helen pressed her hand and said she thought she had been very sensible. "The days of female immolation are past," she said.

"We've decided we're not going to get worked up over those incidents," Oliver announced to Sarah over dinner, on her first full day back. He was treating her with great attention, and talking about any subject but the death of her mother. "Why should we dignify them by taking notice of them? It is the silly season, after all."

"The silly season is newspapers, not people," objected Elizabeth.

"The only reason the newspapers have a silly season is because people do silly things," returned Oliver.

This new resilience was a relief to Sarah, and she decided that they were right. Attention was what the incidents seemed to be crying out for, and what they should not be given. The atmosphere in the house was certainly light and cheerful again. Oliver played ball games on the lawn with Chloe and Bounce, and had lots of friends over for tea. The approach of the Oxford term apparently made him wish for company before the serious business of life began again. Helen made a couple of trips to London to buy clothes, and took Elizabeth with her on one of them. They apparently began scouting round for "some dowager," as Helen put it, to chaperone Elizabeth during her Season. Helen would hardly have liked to do it herself, and as she said, the only people she knew in London were of entirely the wrong sort. Dennis's idea of happiness was being busy, and he was very busy indeed.

"Everyone is dying," he protested, half-humorously. "And I seem to be appointed necrologer. I've no sooner finished a long memorial piece on Housman than they're after me for an article on Lorca. God—poor Lorca. And there's a dreadful spate of books on T. E. Lawrence they expect me to review, presumably because he was brought up in Oxford. Our paths certainly never crossed in Egypt. Oliver would do a much better job, having at least been to these places recently, but they thought that would look like nepotism, and insisted I do it."

Only a postcard from Will dented the gaiety. The very stamp and postmark made Helen go white when she saw it: it had been posted in Barcelona. Will wrote that Madrid itself was under immediate threat, and nobody was taking bets on its remaining in government hands long. There was urgent need for young men with military training to join the anti-Fascist forces. There was talk of an International Brigade. He bitterly regretted not having joined the Officer Cadet Corps at school, but anyway he expected to be ready to fight in a matter of weeks. Already the British volunteers had suffered their first casualties—John Cornford wounded.

"He talks about casualties as if they were a matter of pride," said Dennis Hallam sadly. "As some people talk about having been blooded after a fox hunt."

"Who is this Cornford?" asked Helen. "Should we know?"

"He's a young Cambridge hot-head, made quite a name for himself with the up-and-coming generation. Mistresses—a child, I think. And fancies himself as a poet."

Helen sighed.

"He sounds like the sort of man Will would look up to." She wiped her eyes. "Please God it ends soon."

"It's not going to end soon," said Dennis bleakly.

But they were now quite helpless, and quite unable to influence Will's decisions. From self-protection they put such moments speedily behind them.

Meanwhile the summer was fading, and Sarah learnt that with the turning of the leaves the minds of people in that part of Oxfordshire began turning to the autumn party at the Wadhams'. She had heard of Lord Wadham, whose property began half a mile away, on the other side of the river. People had mentioned him over tea, never with anything less than affection. He was, though, just a name, for he had been involved in none of the visiting over the summer. It was the Hallams who were the "house" people for all the villagers whom Sarah had tentatively begun to talk to. They were all on the Hallams' side of the river, and the Wadhams' greatness, such as it was, was acknowledged in villages on the other bank, to the east. Their house, she had learned, was called Beecham Park, and their party was an annual event.

"The purpose," said Dennis, grinning, for the Wadhams in general seemed to provoke mirth, "is to mark the end of summer, or more accurately to mark the resumption of Parliament. You might think from that that Waddy is a highly political person, but he's not. So far as I know he's attached to no party—he merely attends daily at the House of Lords, and speaks at random on whatever subjects attract him."

"So at random," remarked Oliver, "that I would think any party would pay him *not* to attach himself to it. His speeches would be sublimely embarrassing."

"That only shows how boring and humourless politicians are," said Helen. "They ought to be queueing to sign up such an individual old dear. Waddy in the government would add enormously to the gaiety of nations."

"He's a love," agreed Elizabeth. "I wonder if I should ask Lady Waddy to be my chaperone for the Season."

At this the family collapsed into gales of laughter. The Wadhams, it seemed, were not likely to be formidable hosts. Sarah asked timidly what kind of a party it was to be.

"A fun and games party," explained Oliver. "Monopoly and murder, and croquet on the lawn in the dark— oh, and what else? Piquet, poker, shove ha'penny, and anything else that can be dragged out of the cupboards at Beecham. Waddy will certainly give readings from Dickens at some point—"

"Dickens?"

"That's right. But he doesn't mind if you slip away. Do I gather you are not up in Dickens, Sarah?"

"Not really. I don't remember we even had copies at

home. I've read *Oliver Twist* and *David Copperfield.* Oh, and bits of *Pickwick,* but I never found it as funny as other people seem to."

"Dear me. Well, I don't think Waddy will do 'Death of Nancy' or 'Death of Steerforth.' It's much more likely to be Flora Finching—he has a very good line in Floras —or maybe Harold Skimpole. I would suggest you prepare yourself by reading *Bleak House.*"

"Don't scare Sarah," said Helen. "It's not at all a scary occasion, my dear. The whole and only purpose is for everybody to have fun—in particular Waddy, who needs some lightening of the spirit before he returns to his duties at Westminster."

They all laughed. In fact all the Wadhams seemed to provoke such wholehearted and good-natured mirth that Sarah realized there could be no possible element of the alarming in their forthcoming party. She felt she was beginning to mingle with the great on the easiest possible terms, and under the best possible auspices. Nevertheless she began to read *Bleak House.*

Meanwhile Sarah had a second evening at the pictures with Roland Bradberry. He rang her up at Hallam, and when she asked Mrs. Hallam if she could have Saturday evening off, Helen said she must just say, not ask, because she was on duty practically all the time, and needed relaxation. Sarah felt that it was impossible to imagine duty that was more consistently and stimulatingly pleasant than her work at Hallam, and she smiled and said of course she would always ask.

"You've found a young man," said Helen.

"A young man is taking me," said Sarah cautiously.

"Well, if it becomes serious I hope you'll tell—oh dear, I was going to say I hoped you'd tell your mother. Please forgive me, Sarah dear."

"I certainly won't tell my father unless there is something definite to tell," said Sarah.

"I can understand that," agreed Helen. "I hope if there's anything you want to talk over, you'll come to me. I suppose in a way I'm a stand-in for your mother at the moment."

But Sarah was determined there would be nothing to talk over, for a while, anyway. Life was just beginning. It had, she felt, begun with her coming to Hallam. The exploration of life's possibilities was hardly under way. There were going to be no hasty decisions, no falling into traps, no steps taken in hotness of blood that would close up possibilities for the years ahead.

Meanwhile the excursion to Willbury Village Hall was a nice night out. The film was *Little Women* and it presented fewer excitements than *Grand Hotel.* The audience took it very much in their stride, and this time voiced occasional comments on the plot as the action progressed. It was altogether a less rapt occasion, but Sarah enjoyed it none the less.

In the breakdown they stood a little aside this time, standing against the wall of the village inn. Barry Noaks showed some sign of wanting to approach them again, but at a shake of the head from Roland he stopped some yards away.

"Hear you've got a nigger up at the hall, that right?" he shouted. Sarah found it difficult to respond tactfully at that volume.

"We had an Indian friend of Oliver's. He's gone now."

"What them Hallams want a nigger for?" shouted Barry. But at another sign from Roland he turned and went away. Sarah was glad. She found his loud, crowing vacancy difficult to stomach, and she admired Roland for his tolerance. She turned to him and said in a low voice:

"Which are Major Coffey's star recruits? Are there any of them here?"

Roland looked around.

"That lad over there in the light blue pullover is Bertie Marsh. And the chap next to him is Jim Fallow. I don't think Chris Keene is here—oh, wait: that's him coming out of the shop with an ice-cream."

Sarah looked at them all. None of them looked at all like Barry Noaks. In fact, they not only looked normal, they looked rather lively: the sort who in one way or another are likely to take a lead in village life, be marked out from the general torpidity, whether by being on the parish council or by being the star poacher. Chris Keene even seemed to have a rare quality of gaiety about him. He was obviously a village wit, and kept a little knot of younger members of the audience rocking with appreciative laughter.

"It seems a bit odd . . ." she said hesitantly. "They all seem sort of . . . above average. I mean, not yokels . . ."

Roland laughed.

"You sound like Rector Kroll."

"Who's he? A clergyman?"

"No, a headmaster in Ibsen. He couldn't understand why the radical students who were rebelling against him were all drawn from his brightest boys."

"But this is quite different!" protested Sarah. "These boys are not radical, they're horribly reactionary!"

"Maybe it's just a question of what rebellion happens to be going," said Roland.

The film this time was shorter, and there were fewer villagers there. Their walk home, though very dark, was more solitary and intimate than it had been last time. They were more relaxed with each other too, and were discovering more things to talk about. When the talk shifted from Roland and his prospects after Oxford to Sarah and her plans after the Hallams, Sarah let herself talk and talk, ranging over this and that, so that it might have seemed that the possibilities for her were endless, instead of severely limited (as they were, in fact, for Roland too). They were so close, both physically and temperamentally, that Sarah decided to let Roland kiss her at the gate. She was quite sure he would try to, or ask.

Thus her mind, as they approached the gate—now in fact nothing but gateposts, without either gate or keeper in the tiny lodge beside it—was on the kiss, rather than on the approach of home. It was only when they stopped talking and she turned towards Roland that she noticed something out of the corner of her eye and swung back. Immediately the kiss was forgotten.

Hanging on the gatepost, on the hinge left behind by the removed gate, there was a dead chicken.

"Bloody fools!" said Roland violently, and strode over to take it down.

"No, don't. It may be evidence."

Sarah looked at the unappetizing bird. It had been hung by its head, and its neck seemed an inordinate length. It looked yellow and scaly in the moonlight, and none the pleasanter for being obviously the sort of fowl that would need long, slow cooking.

"Evidence of what?" asked Roland. "I can't see that hanging a chook on a gatepost is any sort of crime. They're being very cunning, don't you see? And I shouldn't think the surface is susceptible to fingerprints."

He looked at it with distaste, and Sarah, after a few moments, decided to giggle.

"It is a bit of an anti-climax after the dog. Poor old bird. Why is a dead dog horrible but a dead hen ridiculous? Actually, the Hallams are wanting to play all this down. They think it's just village foolishness rather than anything worse. I suppose the best thing is to get rid of it. I can have a word quietly with Mr. Hallam and say we've disposed of it."

But barks from the other side of the house told them that Bounce had been let out for his evening run-around. He sensed Sarah in the vicinity, and in a trice was cavorting over the darkened garden to welcome her home. He had no sooner jumped up to greet her than he sensed the chicken and set up a great barking at the instrusive presence. He sat beneath it, protesting, and when Roland tried to take it he redoubled his noise, convinced he was being robbed of something. Soon the front door of the house opened, and a figure appeared against the lighted hall, peering out.

"They're a bit on edge," whispered Sarah. She stood in the gateway and shouted: "It's all right. It's only me, Sarah." She turned to Roland. "I must go." Bounce jumped up at her again, imploring her to prevent his being despoiled of the desirable bird, which would never torment him or fly away as all the other birds did. She took him by the collar. Roland, the bird flung over his shoulder, bent forward, and, tickled by dog fur and the neck feathers of the chicken, they had their first kiss.

"I'm sorry about the bird," whispered Roland.

"It was unlike any kiss I've had," said Sarah. Then, waving with one hand and still clutching Bounce with the other, she darted across the front lawn to the safety of light and home.

When she got in she talked about the film, and it was not until next morning that she told Dennis. He made

light of it, but said that he was calling in on Sergeant
South on his way to Oxford that afternoon, and he'd tell
him then.

"It's another little piece of persecution," he said, "but
it's hardly against the law. Apart from the killing of the
dog, they've kept well inside it. Now it's just pinpricks,
and we just have to wait until they get tired."

With that verdict, apparently, Sergeant South agreed.
Over sherry that evening Dennis told Sarah that the envelope with the white feather had been tested for fingerprints, and the sender was found to be Christopher
Keene. He had been up before magistrates two years before, on a minor pilfering charge. South had had a long,
stern talk with the boy, but he was not particularly san-
guine about its effects.

"We must hope that they run out of metaphors for
cowardice," said Dennis, with a sad smile.

8

———— • ————

They took the Wolseley to the Wadhams' party, because they were all rather decked out. Not exactly in fancy dress, because it wasn't that sort of party, but not normally dressed either. It was for this reason they decided not to walk. They could have gone over the river by the little wooden bridge to the west of Hallam's lawns, and then along a half-mile of country lanes to Beecham Park. But as Helen said: who wanted to make a raree show for the locals? "And what a fag, walking home after all those games!"

There were other, unspoken, reasons for not wanting to walk home in the dark.

They had all rummaged around in the trunks and attics of Hallam to come up with something in the clothing line that would appeal to the Waddies. Amusing the Waddies was apparently the whole aim of this party, which seemed rather topsy-turvy to Sarah when she thought about it. But the trunks were a delight, a miniature history of English clothes over the previous hundred years. Dennis came up with cream boating gear and a straw hat, a get-up which had probably graced Henley around the year 1910. Helen found a long, drapey woollen dress, immediately post-war, three-quarter length and a rather slimy green, and she said she intended to be a Bloomsbury lady. "But darling, you don't look a *bit* like Virginia Woolf!" protested Dennis. "No long, soulful face, and *much* too pretty." And indeed, when she put it on, she looked like a very pretty woman pretending to be Bloomsbury. "I'm sure there *are* pretty Bloomsbury women," said Helen. "We're not far from Bloomsbury people ourselves."

Oliver went as a Victorian blood, Elizabeth found a costume which had been used in amateur theatricals, and which was labelled "Prince Orlofsky." She made a handsome prince. Sarah decided on a weird and wonderful black and purple flowing dress, that must have been left behind by some exotic visitor late in the last century.

"It makes you look like some Rumanian countess," said Helen. "Or did Queen Marie ever stay here, I wonder?"

Chloe looked enchanting in a sailor suit, and not in the least boyish.

Even driving through the country roads to Beecham Park felt a bit odd. "We might be on our way to Mr. Korda's film studio," said Elizabeth. Of course all the country people who saw them knew exactly where they were going. Many of them had been involved in preparing the substantial quantities of food that were to be provided. "Tuck," said Elizabeth, screwing her face up. "Or nursery fare." Drink, apparently, was more sparingly available, and both Dennis and Oliver had provided themselves with hip flasks.

Their reception was very different from that at Cabbot Hall. In fact there was no reception. The party was already under way, and they heard from open doors and windows laughter and shrieks. So the Hallams just got out of the car and went in, hoping at some point to meet their hosts so that they could introduce Sarah. In fact the first people they met that Sarah knew were the Mostyn Hallams. Chloe threw herself joyfully into Winifred's arms, and Sarah could almost feel the conflict of affection and jealousy in the woman. She laughed and cuddled her, then put her back on the ground to run off.

"She's a delightful child," said Sarah.

"Wonderful. Almost too good to be true," said Winifred haltingly. "You're lucky . . . So lucky."

Sarah suddenly found Winifred rather congenial in her gauche openness to hurt. She said, not entirely going off at a tangent:

"I enjoyed your gardens at Cabbot. They're beautifully . . . random, if that's the word, and if it isn't insulting. Are they of your making?"

"Largely. Yes, it was a quite different sort of wilderness when we got the place. Are you interested? Would you like to come and see around properly some time? Not much to see here at Beecham, I'm afraid, even if there were more light. A muddle rather than a wilderness, and not a very creative one. The Waddies are not interested in gardens."

They were still in the entrance hall, the Hallams talking to some other neighbours, people by the name of Cousins, whom Sarah had met over tea at Hallam. He was tall, and handsome in an immensely aristocratic way that Sarah found rather intimidating, while she was small and fluffy and silly. She and Winifred were about to turn and go into the main part of the house, whence all the jollity came, when Winifred said: "Ah—here's Waddy."

Here, in fact, were most of the Waddies.

Waddy himself was a delightful bumbler of a man, dressed in tweed trousers and an old cardigan with leather patches on the sleeves. He might have just come in from feeding the dogs. His wife wore a thick brown jumper, a grey skirt, and ankle socks. They were delighted to see both branches of the Hallams.

"Hello m'dears!" chortled Waddy. "Well, if it isn't the lovely Chloe. You're more beautiful every time I see you, young lady, and if that isn't your mother's influence I don't know what is. Is this your new governess, then? She's a bobby-dazzler like you, isn't she? What are you going to play, Chloe? We've got so many games you won't know where to start. We're just off to find somewhere to set out the Monopoly board."

He handed over the game to one of his daughters. There were two of them, lumpish, amiable girls, incredibly dreary in dress (though Sarah was glad to see that neither of them sported ankle socks), and apparently raring to pile up properties on Mayfair and Park Lane. Their mother watched them go, fondly.

"It's so lucky women are not allowed on the Stock Exchange. We should none of us have any money left."

Waddy had taken Dennis by the arm, confidentially. He apparently regarded him as a sounding-board, a well-disposed critic.

"I say, Hallam, did you know we have a debate on population coming up in the Lords? Listen—I've thought of a phrase, tell me what you think of it. 'What we need is not birth control but self-control.' Rather good, eh?"

"Awfully good, Waddy. But I thought you were rather in favour of birth control?"

"Ah—that was before I thought of the phrase," said Waddy, with a look of beguiling cunning. "What do you think, eh? Will it get me a paragraph in the *Daily Mail?*"

"What a lovely dress, my dear," said Lady Wadham to Sarah. "Is the Eastern look fashionable this year? I must get some nice gauzy scarves and pin them to my jumpers."

"Actually," said Sarah awkwardly, because after all this wasn't supposed to be fancy dress, "it's something we found in a trunk at Hallam, Lady Wadham."

"Well, you all look terribly *fun*, which is the main thing," said Lady Wadham, quite unoffended. "And do call me Josabeth, my dear. Now, do you feel like joining Susan and Jane at Monopoly? They have an absolute craze on it at the moment, I suppose because they have so little money of their own, poor things. Or I wonder what Simon is getting up. Sarah, this is Simon . . . Oh, and this is a friend of Simon's, Major . . ."

"Coffey," said Sarah. "We have met."

She had not seen him, standing silently behind, in the shadow of the staircase, a sinister presence. She shook hands reluctantly, disliking intensely the sardonic half-smile, replete with self-satisfaction, with which he greeted her. Everyone else seemed to have evaporated, and she was forced to turn, *faute de mieux*, back to Simon, the son of the house.

"What is it you're getting up?" she asked.

Simon Killingbeck, the next Lord Wadham, was as unlikely a son of Lord and Lady Wadham as it was possible to imagine. Most probably he was a throwback to his great-grandfather, Jubal Killingbeck, who had made his fortune in the Potteries, manufacturing equipment for public urinals and private privies. A cantankerous old slave-driver he had been, with a nose for money and an itch for power. His punishment in this life was to know that he had handed on his dubious gifts neither to his son nor his grandson, whom he regarded as mentally defective. Lord Wadham still had interests in the family firm, but the direction of it had long since passed to more

capable hands. In Simon the old Adam had disconcert-
ingly reappeared. He was a fair boy, with prominent eyes,
not good-looking, but with a firm, mean mouth and an
obstinate expression that boded ill for anybody and anything that stood in his way.

"Croquet," he said, with no particular invitation in
his voice. Never since she came to the Hallams had Sarah
been told more clearly that she was a nursery governess.

Some obstinate instinct made her say: "I'll play."

He looked at her insolently for a moment, then
turned back into the doorway that led to the rest of the
house.

"Come on, all the croquet players," he shouted.

On the lawn outside the darkness was broken only by
the lights from the house. A little knot of six players
assembled, but they were watched from the wall of the
house by the Major, a saturnine, unfestive presence. Simon introduced Sarah to nobody, and seemed to think it
neither funny nor fun to play croquet in the dark. The
squeals of laughter inside were not reproduced on the
lawn. It was the oddest game of croquet Sarah had ever
played. The near-darkness made it difficult at the beginning to see the hoops. Even when Sarah's eyes had accustomed themselves to the murk, it was not possible to see
all the balls. It became clear after about ten minutes that
Simon Killingbeck's team was the less proficient of the
two. From that moment Sarah was conscious of oddities
in the game—balls, mainly Simon's, that seemed to have
been moved, discrepancies in the scoring, to his advantage.

Others, she felt sure, had noticed too. They did not
protest. Simon was, after all, the son of the house. And of
course they probably knew him better than to protest.
Sarah wondered whether the Major was proud of his pro-

tégé's cunning. As the game was drawing to its close she realized the Major was no longer watching, and wondered which of the laughing groups he was making uneasy by his participation in their fun.

"Thank you for a splendid game," said Sarah to Simon at the end. "It's always stimulating to play with someone who has the will to win."

Inside the house the various festivities were going on with great zest and noise. Sarah looked in on the smallest guests, who were playing Happy Families, which was Chloe's favourite game. In another room the Killingbeck girls were amassing huge sums of paper money at Monopoly, and in the study Waddy was doing his performance from Dickens.

He was standing at a lectern, rather in the manner of late photographs of the author himself, and performing with all the dreadful enthusiasm of the amateur actor.

" 'The African project at present employs my whole time,' " said Waddy, his eye fixed on some distant, unhealthy shore. Ah, so he was doing Mrs. Jellyby. At least Oliver had got the book right. " 'We hope by this time next year to have from a hundred and fifty to two hundred healthy families cultivating coffee and educating the natives of Borrioboola-Gha, on the left bank of the Niger.' "

He had a little knot of listeners, for whom no doubt this was an annual treat, or tour of duty. Probably like most customs this one had become enjoyable after a time. Certainly Lady Wadham seemed to be loving it, and plenty of the others were laughing dutifully. Sarah stood in the doorway for about five minutes, then felt she could slip away.

In the conservatory food had been set out. Most of the guests had been roped in for one game or another, but one or two had managed to resist. Sarah saw Dennis capture Elizabeth on her way from a game of Sardines, looking for another game to join. He was pressing her to some of the fare, and Sarah went over to join them.

The food was less than inviting—but then nobody came to the Waddies for the food, Dennis said. It was, as Elizabeth had prophesied, nursery food, and like nursery food it was lukewarm. There was an awful preponderance of jellies and junkets and tinned fruit with cream, but if one really looked one could find Cornish pasties, cottage pie and macaroni cheese, all kept warm on chafers. Sarah took a dish of kidneys that would have been nice if it had not entirely lacked salt or pepper in the preparation. Dennis and Elizabeth were already deep in a typically Hallam discussion about why mad women wore ankle socks.

"It's an observable phenomenon," insisted Dennis. "And all over the country. Mad women wear socks in Scotland and Wales too."

"Oh, absolutely," agreed Elizabeth. "But does a taste for ankle socks drive you mad, or does madness somehow create a taste for ankle socks?"

"And are all ankle-sock wearers mad, and do all mad women wear ankle socks?" contributed Sarah.

"Ah," said Dennis. "Here we must go carefully. It was our respected hostess who raised the question in our minds. And personally I would contend that Josabeth—"

"I could hardly believe that was her name," said Sarah. "How unfortunate."

"Yes, isn't it? Her father was a church organist with a passion for Handel. The name comes from one of his lesser-known oratorios. Anyway, I would contend that Josabeth, though eccentric, is by no means mad. If we certify her, we would have to certify half the House of Lords."

"That would make the debates much less entertaining," agreed Elizabeth. "Certainly madness requires more than a scatterbrain. It requires obsession. Apropos of which, Sarah, did Major Coffey get hold of you again?"

Sarah screwed up her face.

"We exchanged two words, unavoidably."

"We evaporated when we saw him," said Dennis. "It used to be our policy to be impeccably polite, if cool. I would find it difficult to keep to that, after all this."

"I must say I was surprised to see him here," said Elizabeth. "Not at all the Waddies' type. And what jolly game can one imagine him playing?"

"He seems to be here as Simon Killingbeck's friend," said Sarah. "He stood watching us play croquet, but he didn't join in."

"Have you been playing croquet with the Young Master?" asked Elizabeth, eyebrows raised. "And did he cheat?"

"He did."

"He always does. That's why we never have the Waddies over while he's at home. It's worst in his own home, because you can't say anything."

"It seems so unnecessary," said Sarah. "He made no effort to get the best players in his team."

"You miss the point. If he _won,_ it would merely prove that he was better at croquet. If he wins _by cheating_ it proves that he is cleverer than everybody else. Oliver has declined to play with him for years, and so has Will. They refuse to turn a blind eye to it, and have terrific rows with him . . . Where is Oliver, by the way?"

"Haven't seen him for ages," said Dennis. "He went

in with Chloe to start the young ones off, but since then I haven't seen him. There are so many damned games in so many damned rooms, he could be anywhere."

"You could hide yourself for Sardines and not be found for months," agreed Elizabeth. "I was afraid I'd have to come out, and it'd be a bit like waving the white flag. Oh well, I suppose we'd better get back to the fray. Come on, Aged P."

"Actually," said Dennis, "I'm going to see if there is a little tiny room somewhere that is *not* devoted to board games or card games or ping-pong or billiards. I have a piece to do on D. H. Lawrence and Women, for the Sunday after next. I'm going to curl up with Frieda Lawrence, though I don't think I should like to in real life. *Not I, but the Wind.* Have you ever heard a sillier title? It sounds like an apology for belching."

So Dennis went off in search of a bolt-hole, and Sarah and Elizabeth went in search of some other game to join. They were drawn towards ping-pong, but when they went in the direction of the appropriate sounds, they found that Simon Killingbeck had taken over the table, and was directing a tournament he was surely destined to win. They retreated upstairs, and found themselves welcomed into a game of Murder. All the *nicest* people in the county were involved, Elizabeth whispered, and it certainly seemed that the game attracted a pleasant type.

"I love murder, don't you?" said Winifred Hallam to Sarah. They were waiting around for the next game to start. "I mean detective stories. Mostyn is awful, he says he never guesses them, and sticks with John Buchan and Dornford Yates. But not guessing the murderer is part of the fun, isn't it? Have you read *The ABC Murders?* It's pure heaven, and quite impossible to guess. Actually, I don't like the *game* of Murder quite as much . . ."

Nor, when it came to playing, did Sarah. Probably she would have done, had it not been for the recent incidents. They had made her jumpy—was someone doing something nasty in her vicinity, was she being watched? Murder in an old house rather increased the jumpiness. Mostyn Hallam was the sort of man who entered with an avuncular zest into games of this sort. "Ho-ho," he would say as he strangled someone, "I've wanted to do this for years." Or if he was not the murderer he would enjoy the girls' squeals if he brushed up against them in the dark in a way that Sarah wondered a little about. They only used the first and second floors of Beecham Park, since the ground floor was entirely given over to the various games, but still there was ample area to give Sarah at times a nasty feeling of eeriness, abandon, or—worse—the feeling that she had thought she was alone, but now realized she was not.

All in all Sarah was rather glad when they had finished with it.

"Oh dear," said Winifred, mopping her sweating face. "It's like being a child again. Childhood *is* rather scary, often, isn't it?"

"Nonsense, it was pure fun," said Elizabeth robustly. "I wasn't scared for a moment. I wish I could think we would play games like this during the Season!"

"Elizabeth—are you coming out? How delightful! I never would have guessed you'd do it. You won't regret it. I enjoyed every moment of my coming-out Season . . ."

Helen, whom they had seen little of all evening, was in the hall looking for everyone when they finally went down. She had made the mistake, she said, of getting involved in the second game of Monopoly. By pure luck she had got marvellous properties, and in spite of a valiant struggle by the Killingbeck girls, had won. They had taken their failure rather as their great-grandfather would have taken the bankruptcy of his firm. "They seem to confuse it with real life," said Helen. "It's rather frightening. I would have lost if I'd known . . ."

Anyway, where was everyone?

Chloe, apparently, had insisted on playing Happy Families the entire evening, and had somehow had her way by charm, cajoling or sheer bossiness. Oliver appeared through the front door while they were talking, and said he had been having a practice knock at croquet while the appalling Simon wasn't there to cheat. When Sarah and Elizabeth said that Dennis had intended to go to earth and read a book they organized a Dennis-hunt, and eventually found him in a primitive loo intended for the servants. He had a sheaf of shiny toilet paper covered with scrawl, and he said he had his piece on Lawrence and Women roughed out.

Downstairs was something of a free-for-all, as the party drew to its close. Since the Hallams knew almost everybody there, they had a great many goodbyes to say. When Mostyn and Dennis shook hands the former said:

"Remember what we were talking about last time we met, Dennis? You mark my words, the King's Matter will be out in the open before Christmas at the latest."

"Mostyn, Will is fighting in Spain," said Dennis, with traces of irritation. "I'm really not very interested in the King's Matter."

"Oh, sorry, old man. I forgot. Bad business. Worse than I thought. But I'm sure it will all die down."

Waddy and Lady Waddy had disentangled themselves from their various games, and they stood at the door to wave their guests goodbye, spooning junket into their mouths all the while. "Spiffing fun," said Waddy, kissing the ladies of the party, and shaking hands with the men. "Top-hole," responded Dennis. "Your Mrs. Jellyby was marvellous."

As the car drove off Sarah waved to them in the square of light in the middle of the façade. Behind them in the hallway she spotted Simon Killingbeck and the two lumpish girls. In the driveway people were milling around, saying farewells and finding their cars. And in a patch of light under an oak tree she saw the figure of Major Coffey, surveying their departure from beneath bushy, overhanging eyebrows.

They were all quite boisterous on the way home. They agreed they'd had a gorgeous time, and it was really lovely to let your hair down once in a while and be a child again. Dennis drove through the ink-black darkness, and left the car by Hallam's main entrance. There was nothing on the gatepost, nothing on the front door. Sarah did, when she pulled her bedroom curtains, think she saw an odd light, at the far end of the lawn as it dipped down towards the river. But she decided it was a trick of moonlight, and didn't think to investigate further.

Thus it was Pinner the manservant, early next morning, who found the body that was to change the course of Sarah's life at Hallam.

9

It was nearly forty years after she left Hallam before Sarah visited it again. By then it was a National Trust property, and she got in free with her member's card. She had one of her grand-daughters with her, and she walked around the house with something like apprehension in her heart. But all the old, family furniture of the Hallams' time had gone, replaced by solid Elizabethan and Jacobean pieces. Where Helen's picture by Sir Philip de Laszlo had used to hang in the hall, a be-ruffed and bearded gentleman stared belligerently out. Her grandchild was bored, and Sarah felt alien. It was like visiting present-day Bucharest with memories of the pre-war city —different in essence, however similar the frame might be. When the little girl tugged at her hand and pointed through the windows at the lawn, Sarah did not resist.

The grounds, at least, were largely the same, and though the grand-daughter was plump and serious, the sight of her running across the lawn brought a lump to Sarah's throat as she remembered the beauty of the child Chloe. (Chloe, whom she lunched with once a month in Soho, plump, nicotine-stained, and working for the *Sunday Times* colour magazine, a job which Sarah thought was beneath her.) The little signposts directing visitors to the Adventure Playground and the Garden for the Blind were a distraction at first, but as she strolled over the lawns, almost alone in the May sunshine, the familiar magic reasserted itself and she felt an incredible peace. It was only when the little girl ran towards a weeping willow, silver-yellow with its new leaves, that a lump rose in her throat and she felt the urge to shout "No!" and run and gather her up in her arms.

She repressed the urge, of course. Why frighten the mite? Why feel fear herself? She forced herself to walk after the little girl in the direction of the willow, forced herself to stand where she remembered the body to have lain. There was no bloodstain. Naturally there was no bloodstain. The new grass grew lustily. She reproved herself: she was a woman of the twentieth century, above such foolish fancies. Nevertheless, when she saw her grand-daughter galloping down the bank towards the river, her quickened step was not caused by fear for her safety alone.

There was not a lot of blood to be seen, even on that October morning in 1936.

Sarah awoke around eight, conscious there had been barking. There was a nip in the air, and she thought she would soon accept Mrs. Munday's offer of one of the stone hot-water bottles that hung in the kitchen. Then she heard voices below her window, and she felt sure they were not the voices of any of the jobbing gardeners who came in regularly from the villages. Anyway, today was Sunday. She drowsed on a bit, registering that Bounce was barking again, this time from inside the house.

Still there were voices, men's, but now they were from

further away. A sense of unease invaded her, and she got up and went to the window.

The voices came from the far end of the great lawn, from beside the weeping willow that was Sarah's favourite tree in the grounds. It was a long way away, too far for Sarah to be quite sure who the figures were. That surely was Pinner, not yet dressed for the day, for he certainly had no jacket on, and Sarah could picture him as she had sometimes seen him in the early morning, with braces on, and without collar and tie. The other figure—was it Oliver? Or was it Dennis? That looked like an old sports jacket Dennis sometimes wore around the house. And there was a third figure, on the ground . . . not getting up. Sarah shivered.

And there was something else too. She strained her eyes. Something that glowed . . . *Glowed?* As she drew the curtains to, the figures on the lawn seemed to finish their conference. They turned and began to hurry towards the house.

Sarah quickly gathered together her clothes for the day. In a couple of minutes she was dressed and slipping out on to the landing and down the broad wooden staircase. Pinner had unlocked and unchained the front door —good. She would certainly be intercepted if she went through the kitchens. Why she wanted to see what was there by the willow tree she could not have said, but she was a girl who had always believed in facing up to the worst—evaluating and assimilating it. Her upbringing had done that for her, at any rate. Now she had an instinctive feeling that life at Hallam was never to be the same again.

She hurried across the lawn, not running, feeling that would be wrong, or undignified. She was headed towards the weeping willow, not trying to make out what was nearby it. As she gained the further stretches she heard a shout. She turned. On the balustrade of the formal garden Pinner was calling to her, gesturing to her to come away. She stood her ground, and then looked back towards the leafy willow.

The strangest component of the grotesque little tableau was the object that had caused the glow which Sarah had noticed from her bedroom window. It was a lifesize reproduction of a human skeleton, made with some kind of light wood, and painted with a silvery, phosphorescent paint. It was the sort of scary-funny object that might be obtained in any joke shop, particularly now, with the approach of Hallowe'en. The skull glistened blankly up to the morning sky, the trunk lay outstretched in the posture of death. Except, Sarah noted almost subconsciously, that the backbone had been painted out.

The young man, dead beside it, was less formally laid out. The body was also on its back, but more higgledy-piggledy, apparently because he had died in the course of a struggle, or some violent exertion of some kind, and had been left where he was. There was a hole in his forehead, and the back of his head . . . Sarah could hardly bear to look at the back of his head . . . But she registered a little patch of blood on the grass, and wondered that such a terrible wound had not produced more. She turned away from the sight, feeling sick.

"We tried to stop you seeing it," said a voice behind her. It was Dennis, looking haggard and unwell.

"I prefer to know the worst," said Sarah. "I could see there was something wrong as I was getting up . . . It's grotesque. That ridiculous skeleton, yet with real death beside it."

"He'd painted out the backbone," said Dennis, his

voice low and hollow. "I was a fool to think they'd ever run out of metaphors for cowardice."

He put his arm out to lead Sarah away, but she forced herself to turn back.

"I think I've seen him," she said, her voice almost reduced to a whisper. "Who is he?"

"One of the village lads."

"I think I saw him, the last time I went to the pictures in Willbury . . . Was it Christopher Keene?"

"That's who Pinner thought it was."

Sarah let herself be gently led away by him, back towards the house.

"We know what he was doing, or planning to do," she said, trying to get her voice back to normal. "If only we could work out how it could have happened."

"It could have been an accident," said Dennis.

If only it could! If only it could!

"Then where is the gun?" asked Sarah, her voice sounding harsh.

"I know, I know. But he could have had a friend . . . an accomplice. They could have been horsing around."

It was a possibility Sarah had not considered.

"And when the gun went off and killed him, this friend who was helping him took fright and ran away, still holding the gun. Yes, it could have happened like that. But the gun would be terribly incriminating."

"The friend might not be very bright."

"Barry Noaks," said Sarah, her voice flat, but with something like hope in it.

"Is he the idiot boy from Chowton?" Dennis thought for a few moments. "It's possible."

"But why in any case bring a gun?" Sarah asked. "Were they planning something else?"

"You mean direct violence against one of us? It doesn't seem to go with the practical joke."

"Barry Noaks seems to be obsessed with dead things," said Sarah, shivering. "He seems to enjoy the idea of blood."

"We mustn't jump to conclusions. The police will have all the scientific means to find out, and the experience. If it's possible to get at the truth, they'll get there, and we must leave it to them . . . And if I'm not mistaken, this will be them now."

A black Morris Oxford was driving through the gates, and up towards the entrance to Hallam.

"I'll go and talk to them," said Dennis. "Will you take charge of Chloe and shield her from some of this? I think it would be best if she didn't have breakfast with the family. We can hardly avoid the subject."

Best she didn't have breakfast in the kitchen either, Sarah thought. Mrs. Munday and Pinner would regard it as a dreadful intrusion into their discussion of the subject. Constantly busy though they were, they did dearly love to chew over a piece of gossip, if one came up. When she got back upstairs she found that Chloe had already dressed herself, so Sarah installed her in the little schoolroom and fetched a light breakfast for the two of them on a tray. She found it was as much as she could do to toy with a piece of toast, and Chloe, bright as always, noticed her lack of appetite.

"Desks are for writing on, not for eating breakfast on," she announced. "Why are we eating breakfast here?"

"To keep out of everybody's way," answered Sarah.

"Why today? Why do we have to keep out of everybody's way *today*?"

"There's been a spot of bother."

Chloe bided her time. She could be a thinking, watching, waiting child when she wanted to be. When the tray had been put outside the door, and Sarah had set her to copying sentences from a spelling book, she was ready to attack again.

"What *sort* of bother is it there's been a spot of?"

The very complexity of the sentence showed her to be a Hallam. Sarah was standing at the window watching the little knot of men at the far end of the lawn. Only two had come in the Morris Oxford, but now they had been joined by more—trilby-hatted men, one of whom was setting up tripods and unloading photographic equipment. Sarah thought how very unglamorous police detectives were. Then she thought: She'll have to be told something soon.

"There's been an unfortunate accident," she said carefully.

"What sort of accident? A motor accident?"

"No, not a motor accident."

"What sort, then?"

"There was a young man trespassing in the grounds last night."

"While we were at the Waddies'? Tres-passing is when you go on other people's land, isn't it?"

"That's right."

"Tres-passing is not an accident."

"Unfortunately the young man had an accident."

"Is he dead? Or is he just wounded?"

Sarah believed in telling the truth to children.

"I'm afraid he's dead."

Chloe took it quite calmly.

"I know all about death. Grandmother Fawcett died, and Uncle Edward in the Great War. That was before I was born. But I know about dying."

She seemed entirely satisfied, though it would probably not be long before she had thought up more questions. Now, at any rate, she was concentrating on her copying, and Sarah took the chance to skip downstairs.

When she walked into the breakfast-room she found the Hallams slumped over the table in gloomy conversation. She had never known them so dreary. Even Elizabeth was quite without sparkle. They had never gone in for the lavish country house breakfast, but today they seemed to have eaten practically nothing. They accepted Sarah as a natural part of any family conference.

"I've talked to Sergeant South," said Dennis. "He confirms that it is Christopher Keene."

"Yes," said Sarah flatly. "I thought it was. I knew he was involved in these silly pranks, but when I saw him at the pictures—" she struggled to explain—"he seemed . . . such a lively young man. Very bright. It's quite dreadful."

"I'll go and visit his mother," said Oliver quietly. "I know her a little. I helped her fill out a form to get money from the Foresters when his father died."

"Wasn't his father a bit of an invalid?" asked Helen.

"Yes. He'd been gassed in the War. He did farm work, but he'd never really recovered. I know Mrs. Keene had some help from the British Legion too."

"Do go and talk to her," said Dennis. "But perhaps not yet. There'll be an awkwardness, in the circumstances. It beats me how a lively boy, and one whose father was ruined by war, could fall victim to a charlatan like Major Coffey."

Sarah remembered Roland's remark, and adapted it a little.

"Perhaps he offered a bit of excitement. A sort of

escape from the humdrum. There's not much for a lively young person in a village, even in these days."

"No . . ." Dennis thought. "Perhaps we should have understood that. Perhaps we live too much in books."

"Is it known when it happened?" asked Sarah. "Was it when we were at the Waddies'?"

"We'll have to wait for the police doctor's report before we can know that," said Oliver.

"Well, in fact I think we can have a good idea," said Helen. They all looked in her direction. "I've been talking to Mrs. Munday. You know it was Pinner's night off last night, so she was in the house alone until well after the pubs closed. She was going to listen to a light music programme with Gwen Catley at ten, and she said Bounce began to get restless just before that. Barking, wagging his tail, going to the door—'let me get at them,' you know the way he is. Finally she let him out, and he went out on to the parapet above the lawn and barked into the darkness—down towards the river. As usual, as soon as he's allowed to get at them he doesn't dare to. Eventually, she called him in, but he was very restless for the rest of the evening. I think that must have been the time when . . ."

Her voice faded into silence.

"Very likely," agreed Dennis.

"But not conclusive," said Elizabeth. "It could have been a stray cat, or a squirrel."

"Did she hear a shot?" asked Sarah.

"No. But her hearing's not very good, and it was some way away from the kitchen, and on the other side of the house."

"If it agrees with the police doctor's conclusion," said Dennis, "then we can be pretty sure that was when it happened, or about then. But the doctor may not be at all definite. If he had seen the body earlier he probably could have been, but—what?—twelve hours or more have gone by. Knowing doctors, I suspect he will probably be very vague."

The prospect of the police doctor being quite open about the time of the murder, of the whole period of their visit to the Waddies being in question, maybe even the night-time after their return home, depressed the Hallams still further, and made them silent. Sarah murmured that she must see to Chloe, and slipped out and upstairs. As she went she was thinking: ten o'clock. What was I doing at ten o'clock? She must have finished the game of croquet with Simon Killingbeck. Was she playing Murder? Or was she talking to Elizabeth and Dennis over the array of nursery foods? That at any rate would mean that three of them were out of the running. Except that it might have been a cat or a stray squirrel.

And what on earth did she mean—out of the running?

Out on the lawn, a little way away from the posse of men in trilby hats and raincoats, Sergeant South was talking in low tones to Inspector Minchip.

Minchip, to an outside observer, was much the less impressive figure of the two. Three or four inches shorter, lean almost to the point of weediness, he had a ferrety face and a straggling moustache that did nothing for it. Only a steely glint in the eyes and an air of being accustomed to command might suggest that he was a man very much on top of his job. His clothes would have suggested that this was a job which, at the time, Society did not feel called upon lavishly to reward. Notwithstanding that, Sergeant South treated him with immense respect.

"Dr. Bailey isn't committing himself," Minchip was

saying. "He never does if he can help it, not at this stage —and precious little later on. All I've got from him so far is that he doesn't think it could have been committed much later than two a.m. As to the earlier time, he's holding out entirely. So let's say he was killed some time in the evening, or the early part of the night. Now, continuing on from your account of these daft tricks, why was he *here?* The family didn't walk to Beecham Park, and apparently had never said they intended to."

"As to that," said South, "I doubt this was where he intended laying the thing out. That would have been by the front door, or somewhere else where they'd have been bound to see it when they drove home. Either he stopped for a rest—because this skeleton contraption would be very difficult to carry in the dark without damaging it— or he was stopped in his tracks by the dog, and put this little bit o' horror down carefully to avoid damaging it."

"Fair enough," agreed Minchip. "Or just possibly was stopped in his tracks by someone whom he had every reason to believe was a friend. Now, we take it, do we, that he was taking the river path from the village rather than the road? And that he was coming that way because there was little or no chance of his being seen?"

"That's it, sir. Deserted at that time of night it would have been. There was a torch in his pocket which he probably stopped using once he got in sight of the big house."

"You say there was moonlight."

"There was, sir. Near a full 'un."

"So he was on his way to the house, and for one reason or another he paused—laying that silly skeleton out to avoid damaging it. Next question: was he alone?"

"That's a big one, isn't it, sir?"

"You're going to have to make use of all your contacts in the village, South."

"Aye, sir. But you know what villagers are like. A bit of gossip gets round like wildfire, but if they want to protect one of their own, they can clamp up like they had padlocks on their silly mouths."

"You think they'll want to protect their own?"

"Couldn't say, sir. I'll find out soon enough. Unpredictable, that's what folk around here are. My guess would be, anyway, that he was on his own. Or thought he was."

The Inspector turned, interested.

"Why do you say that?"

South pondered, in his slow way.

"Seems to me, sir, these pranks were something in the nature of an initiative test. Each lad given something to do. And I think it'd be on his own. That way it'd be much less likely to be brought home to the real instigator."

"Coffey?"

"Oh, I don't have much doubt about that, personally."

"Yes. We've got a file on him—mostly stuff sent to us from the Metropolitan Police, about his activities in London back in the 'twenties. Seems like he's pretty good at wriggling out from under."

"Even if he warn't on his own, there's no guarantee it was the other one who did it," South pointed out. "If they were . . . confronted, like, the other could have panicked and run."

"Confronted by someone with a gun?"

"Maybe," said South hesitantly.

"These landowners are pretty protective still, even in these days."

"Hardly the Hallams, sir. The present Mr. Hallam has often refused to prosecute poachers caught on his farms. Some of the tenants are quite bitter about it. Anyway they were all at Beecham Park."

The Inspector raised his eyebrows.

"The bridge over the river is not more than a hundred yards away."

"But to come from Beecham *with a gun,* sir. The Wadhams are not sporting people . . . Though the young chap there *has* done a bit of shooting, now I come to think about it."

"And any country house *has* guns. There's always been a sporting man there in the past. Whether in good nick or not is another matter. At the moment I can't see for the life of me why Christopher Keene should have had a gun with him. Damned awkward thing to carry, if he was on his own, and had the skeleton as well."

"As to that, sir, the Major's a military man, and he probably presented these tests to the boys as something in the nature of a military manoeuvre. Sort of incursion into enemy territory."

"Bloody fool. But you're probably right. Sound suggestion."

Sergeant South glowed, mildly. He had another idea as to why Chris Keene should have brought a gun, but for the moment he was keeping it to himself. He had, in many ways, the soul of a villager.

10

———— ● ————

"I offered him a room in this house to use," said Dennis suddenly during breakfast next morning.

"Sorry. Offered who what?" said Helen, looking up from crumbling her toast.

"I offered the Inspector—what's his name?—the use of a room in this house for the investigation. Of course he refused."

"Why 'of course'?" asked Elizabeth.

"Because we're suspects."

"Oh come, Father," protested Oliver.

"I should have realized. We must get used to the fact. Naturally we're under suspicion. We were being persecuted, and we fought back. That's one of the possibilities the Inspector has to consider."

"Nobody who knew us could believe that," said Helen.

"The Inspector does not know us—and it's quite right that he shouldn't. I should hardly like to be exonerated by someone who's a family acquaintance. In point of fact he was quite short with me when he turned down my offer. Obviously I had offended against police etiquette in some way or other."

"And where does police etiquette say that the inquiry *should* be held?" asked Elizabeth.

"In the police station at Chowton. It will be very cramped and inconvenient. It's also Sergeant South's home, after all. Haven't the Souths got children?"

"Two, quite young," said Oliver.

"Well, no doubt something will be improvised. Anyway, at some point in the day he will want to see all of us."

"Including me?" asked Sarah.

"Oh yes. All of us who were at the Waddies'. So let's all try and remember as much as we can about the evening, what we were doing, and what other people were doing. And *please* let's not try to prevaricate or sidestep the truth. We have to get to the bottom of this ghastly business as soon as possible."

Everyone nodded, Sarah among them, and as Dennis threw down his napkin Mrs. Munday put her head around the door.

"Is it all right if I clear away now, Mrs. Hallam? I've got a lot of cleaning and dusting to do this morning. Mrs. Puncheon won't be coming in today."

Mrs. Puncheon was one of the three cleaners who came in on various days of the week to keep Hallam looking presentable.

"Oh, I'm sorry," said Helen. "Is she ill?"

"She sent her apologies," said Mrs. Munday, busying herself at the table. "She's a friend of Mrs. Keene's."

At the time her words produced only the faintest of clicks in Sarah's mind. Later she was to see them as her first intimation of the start of something.

"That was the beginning of the end for your parents," she said one day in 1967, during one of her regular lunches with Chloe in La Bella Isola, in Romilly Street.

Chloe, plump and mini-skirted, was smoking between her soup and her main course.

"I've always hated villages," Chloe said, puffing as she looked around to see who was there. "God, how I hated Poolton Lacey. Richard insisted that we rent his aunt's cottage there, while he wrote his thesis on Robert Musil. My God—the looks, the gossip, the narrowness! It was that village that broke up my marriage."

"Probably," Sarah ventured, "the marriage wouldn't have lasted forever."

"Heavens above! I should hope not," Chloe giggled, a sound like champagne going down a plug. "I don't think I was made for marriage . . . Probably I was made for adultery." She looked down at her ample expanse. "Nowadays I'm not even made for that."

It was that rapturous giggle, filling all corners of the little restaurant, that reminded Sarah of the child Chloe.

"As a matter of fact you loved Chowton when you were a girl," she said. "And knew all about it."

"Villages are fine for small children," said Chloe, stubbing out her Rothmans as the veal approached. "As their minds expand, they need expanded surroundings. I've never liked Chowton whenever I've gone back to it. Give me Hampstead village any day!"

Sarah, who still, after three decades, felt herself perched uncomfortably in London, wished she could agree.

At the time Mrs. Munday's words caused only the faintest of reverberations in her brain. As the cereal bowls and toast racks were cleared away, the family began dispersing for a difficult day. Things became no easier when, in the hall, Pinner handed them another postcard from Will in Barcelona.

* * *

The headquarters that Inspector Minchip had set up in
Sergeant South's square, bare, ugly little council house
was indeed inconvenient. Sergeant South's normal office,
where people from the villages came to notify him of lost
dogs or bicycle lamps, cheeky children and stripped fruit
bushes, now served as a waiting-room. Sergeant South's
living-room now became the interview room, and under
the Sergeant's supervision his wife had removed from it
as far as possible all traces of family life, so that it looked
bare and comfortless. She had lodged the children for the
time being with her sister in Hatherton, and she felt
sorely tempted to decamp there herself, if the case was to
go on for long.

Inspector Minchip did not sigh for headquarters in
some little-used corner of Hallam. Quite apart from the
unorthodoxy of the suggestion, he would not have felt at
home there. His professional life was spare, chill and
cheerless, and he was perfectly happy for his physical
surroundings to suit. His imaginative life revolved
around colourful historical novels such as *Anthony Ad-
verse* and *Captain Hornblower,* but his imaginative life
cast no shadow over his professional one. He was never
tempted to buckle a swash.

If he had had his way, and a car, he would have liked
to travel around and interview the people concerned in
their home settings—at Hallam, at Beecham, or at Cabbot Hall. This not because he would have felt at home
there, but because the suspects would. A relaxed suspect,
in command of his world, is a careless one. Here none of
them would feel at home: it was too bare and hard. The
villagers would be tongue-tied because they were in a
police station, the gentry would feel awkward because
they were in a working man's home. But there was no

help for it. The car in which he had arrived at Hallam
was the only one possessed by the force at Banbury,
where Minchip served, and it had been recalled for use by
the Superintendent. It was always needed for use by the
Superintendent. Minchip might have been able to secure
the use of a motor bicycle, it was true, but he disliked the
machines and distrusted his ability to fix one of them if
anything went wrong. Otherwise there was the bicycle,
which took time. Best, on the whole, to call people in to
No. 7 Hopper Lane, Chowton.

It had to be Dennis Hallam first. Though Minchip
would have liked to have saved him, to have got the feel
and savour of the Oxfordshire gentry of these parts first
before coming to its most famous representative, it had to
be Dennis first. If he and everyone else were not being led
up a blind alleyway by a monstrous red herring, the case
had to revolve around Dennis Hallam. Minchip had
heard Dennis giving thoughtful talks on matters of cur-
rent moment on the Home Service. He had even read
some of his reviews, when staying with his sister (she and
her husband were both teachers of vaguely progressive
outlook, who took the *Observer*). But Minchip was nervous of Dennis. He hoped the man had nothing to hide,
because he feared that the Hallam intelligence and charm
might be more than a match for him if he had.

"This is a terrible business," said Dennis, looking
around him as he was ushered into the room as if he were
a clergyman doing a spot of poor visiting and checking
whether the roof was leaking. "Are you any further with
it?"

"A little, a little," said Minchip, not willing to let this
become an inquisition of himself. "But I expect this to be
a case that takes time. Do sit down, sir."

Dennis sat on the other side of the dining table, facing

Minchip with his battery of files and notepads. "Like being back in the headmaster's study," he told them at Hallam later.

"Now," said Minchip, "I've got the general idea of what you were doing on Saturday night. You were all—including the little girl—at a party at Lord Wadham's. I've heard of him, from odd little items in the popular press, but I've never met the gentleman. I gather this party was—how shall I put it?—sporty. Lots of games and so on."

"That's right. Like a big Christmas party for the district," said Dennis. His face became thoughtful. "It's odd, isn't it? Coffey—or *someone*—plays these childish practical jokes on us, and we go away and play childish games at Beecham Park. Is the world reverting to infantilism?"

"But this party was something of a tradition, I gather."

"Oh yes. Happens every year. And very enjoyable."

"So you knew about it well in advance?"

"Certainly. It's always a weekend or two before Parliament resumes."

"And everyone in the district would know about it too?"

"Oh yes. Many of the village people would have been helping with the preparations. The Waddies don't have a great deal of money, not these days, but this is the social event of their year. There's lots of cooking to be done, and some of the men help with setting up the games in the garden."

"Games in the dark?"

"Sounds odd, but yes. The Waddies would play cricket in the dark if they thought it would be fun."

"I see. And you all went in the car?"

"Yes. The Wolseley."

"Arriving when?"

"Oh, quarter, half past seven."

"You can't be more definite than that?"

"I'm afraid not. Mrs. Munday was listening to the wireless when we left, so she may have a better idea of the time. I should think it takes about ten minutes to drive to Beecham."

"And when you got there, what did you do?"

"Let me see . . . The other Hallams were there—my cousin Mostyn, the MP. And we said hello to the Cousinses, neighbours from across the border in North-amptonshire. Then the Waddies came along, and I caught sight of Major Coffey. I made myself scarce, and I think most of my family did."

"Ah . . . How well do you know the Major?"

"Quite as well as I wish to . . . I knew *of* him before he moved to Chowton, of course. Just from little paragraphs in the newspapers, but after the rise of Mussolini one noticed such things. Then one forgot about him when Mosley formed his British Union. But the next thing one knew he was *here.*"

"You bumped into him in the village?"

"Well, no. I don't have a great deal of call to go into the village. I think I heard he had moved here first. Then someone—maybe Oliver—pointed him out from the car."

"Did you ever meet him socially?"

"I'm afraid so. My cousin Mostyn has these 'do's,' periodically, keeping the constituency sweet, and he started inviting Coffey. I blame him very much. You can't keep people like that too much at arm's length."

"So you have spoken to him?"

"Yes. Briefly. Our policy was to be perfectly polite, and to avoid him as much as possible."

"You don't think anything you did roused his resentment in any way?"

"No, I don't. I don't think it was ever possible for the Major to like us, nor would I want him to. You're trying to say the dislike was social. I'm sure it was political . . . I also think the man is slightly mad."

"Your paths didn't cross at the Wadhams'?"

"No. I made sure of that. Once I was willing to be coldly polite. Now the situation had changed, and I wasn't sure I wanted to be even that any longer."

"So what in fact did you do?"

"During the evening? I've been trying to remember, and I have to some extent, but the trouble is that at do's of this kind one doesn't look at one's watch. Even if one wants to, one fears one of one's hosts might see. So my memories are all a bit vague. I looked in to see if Chloe—that's our youngest child—was all right, but Oliver was in with the small ones, getting together two or three card games, so I wasn't needed. I went looking for Sarah, that's Chloe's nursery governess, who's new. I thought she might be feeling awkward or out of things, but she was out on the lawn playing croquet, and seemed all right. Major Coffey was watching, so there was no inducement to stay. I came in and slipped into Waddy's reading—"

"His what, sir?"

"His recital, whatever you like to call it. He gives a reading from Dickens every year. It's a well-established custom at these parties. He regrets the passing of the reading-aloud habit, and anyway it's a boost to his ego. He has a perfectly harmless desire to perform."

"What work of Dickens was he reading from, sir?"

"*Bleak House*. Mrs. Jellyby while I was there. He may have gone on to something else later—I thought I'd done my duty after ten minutes or so. Then—let me see —I thought there might be Murder going on upstairs—"

"I beg your pardon, sir?"

"The *game* of Murder, man. It's great fun, but I suppose it wouldn't be up your street. Anyway, I thought they might be playing it upstairs, but when I got there it was just Sardines. Elizabeth—that's my other daughter— was playing, but she looked as if she was tired of it. It can be slightly spooky, hiding away in dark places, and all my family is a bit jumpy at the moment, for obvious reasons."

"Quite natural, sir."

"So I waited for her down in the Conservatory and took her off for something to eat. We were joined there by Sarah, who'd finished her game of croquet. I'm pretty sure that was about ten past nine."

"You looked at your watch, sir?"

"Yes. None of the Waddies was around, and I was wondering—"

"How soon you could go home, sir?"

"Well, yes, to be honest."

"You weren't enjoying yourself, sir?"

"Well . . . Trouble is, anything you say about an occasion of this kind is likely to sound priggish, or killjoy. But it's not really my kind of party. Enough is definitely enough."

"But you could hardly leave at ten past nine, sir."

"No. When we'd eaten—about nine-thirty, I imagine —I slipped away. I had a book in my pocket, and I had a hip flask as well. Wine is in short supply at the Waddies, and spirits non-existent. They assume you want Cherryade or Ovaltine. I found a small room, a lavatory for the maids, and sat there reading and writing until from the sounds I heard I guessed that people were beginning to go."

"I see . . . Could you describe this room to me?"

"Well, a loo is a loo, even a servants' one . . ."

"Its position, sir."

"Oh, the second floor, in a corner of the east wing."

"And nobody knew you were there? Nobody interrupted you?"

"No. They don't, do they, in a loo? There was a lock on the door, and though the tide of Murder—the *game,* you know, they played it after Sardines—occasionally rolled in my direction, nobody tried the door."

"So you were unaccounted for during the later part of the evening?"

"Entirely, I'm afraid. By the time I came down I had my article written, and I should think I showed it to my family, but of course that's not evidence, even though it *was* written on toilet paper. I could have had it written before I went to Beecham."

"Quite, sir. You appreciate the way my mind is forced to work," said Minchip, adding to himself: and you've read a few detective stories. He went on. "Now, as to coming home, sir. Would you have any idea of the time you all came away?"

"Yes, to some extent. I looked at my watch as I came out of the loo. It was half past eleven. People had come looking for me, but there was a bit of delay, finding everybody, and saying goodbyes, and so on. But it can't have been much later than midnight when we got home. Pinner and Mrs. Munday had gone to bed, I know that, because Sarah made us all a good night drink in the kitchen while Helen put Chloe to bed. I should think we were all in bed by half past midnight."

"Not to wake again until—?"

"Until Pinner called me in the morning and said there was something funny on the lawn. I knew then it was another of the Major's stupid and nasty tricks. I couldn't have guessed . . ."

"Quite, sir. This boy, Christopher Keene—did you know him?"

"No . . . I mean, if I'd seen him I would have known he was a boy from one of the villages. But I wouldn't have been able to put a name to him."

"And his mother?"

"No, though she may have worked at Hallam now and then, substituting for one of the regulars. That happens quite often. My son knows her better."

"So there can be no question, to your mind, of anything personal in this, on the boy's part."

Dennis shook his head vigorously.

"No, Inspector, absolutely not. I'm quite certain we've done no injury to the Keene family." He pushed back his chair and said bitterly: "We've never had enemies in the villages—until that damned Major arrived."

II

— ● —

They didn't discuss their interviews with Inspector Minchip, not in any real way. Why not, Sarah wondered? They said they'd found it difficult to remember, they said he seemed to know his job, without being anything as positive as nice or nasty. But they didn't talk about what they'd said, about what he'd asked them. They didn't compare notes. Twice Sarah caught Dennis looking at Helen with an interrogation in his eyes. If Helen answered him in any way, the answer escaped Sarah. It was all so unlike the Hallams, so open, so conversational, so unafraid to talk about themselves and their problems.

The next day began badly. Dennis had been scheduled later in the week to give a broadcast talk on "What is Expressionism?" He had always been very good at making ideas and artistic movements understandable to the man in the street. Sarah had been looking forward to hearing on the wireless someone she actually knew. Then, that Tuesday morning, Dennis got a postcard from the BBC saying they had postponed the talk, knowing he would not, in the circumstances, feel like giving it.

"Those *bloody* BBC people!" Dennis said, throwing the postcard violently across the breakfast table. "A few paragraphs in the popular press about a dead body being found on my lawn and, hey presto, they've decided they'd better distance themselves from me. Can't have the BBC being associated with anybody questionable, oh goodness me no! It's that bloody fool John Reith. God! To think of the influence that one man wields! It's like being ruled from the Manse!"

"You could write an article on it," suggested Oliver.

Dennis laughed, his anger evaporating.

"And never be asked back to broadcast again? It would be a heavy penalty. Like most broadcasters, I do rather like the sound of my own voice. But you could be right. It might be worth it."

It was possible to see the shape of an article in the *Observer* forming itself in Dennis's mind.

Later, as they were finishing breakfast, Oliver said:

"I think I should go and visit Mrs. Keene today."

"Wouldn't it be better to go after someone is charged?" Dennis asked. "It would make the atmosphere less awkward."

"I have to go back to Oxford at the end of the week, unless the police insist on my presence here. Anyway, what I really want to see is whether she is in any want. I suppose the boy was the breadwinner. If we're going to be of any use we must get in early."

"Yes, do find out what we can do for her," said Helen. "Make it clear we don't blame her in any way."

"I have to go and buy a birthday card for my father," said Sarah. "If I can get Chloe settled to something we could walk to the village together."

"Good," said Oliver. "I shan't go till eleven or so. Give Mrs. Keene a chance to get the house straight."

Chloe was rather drowsy that morning. She had slept badly, and probably had been affected by the tensions in

the house. She was quite amenable to being sat at a table
in the corner of the kitchen with drawing pad and crayons and the cat on the table watching her. Mrs. Munday
was worked off her feet, with another of the village
women having defected, but she was delighted to have
Chloe with her. Sarah and Oliver set off for the village
soon after eleven.

"I'm not looking forward to this," Oliver confessed.

"Why? Is she an unpleasant woman?" asked Sarah.

"No, no, not at all. Quite a fat, comfortable woman.
Has a dog and two cats who are fed to within an inch of
their lives."

"Why, then?"

"What does one say to a person who has lost everything? First the husband, and now the son. There are no
other children. What has she got to look forward to but
dragging out the rest of her life on a tiny pension? She's
not an old woman, either . . . There's not a lot of cheer-
ing-up things one can think of to say to her."

"Not a lot," admitted Sarah.

She darted a look at Oliver's worried face. It struck
her suddenly how very good Oliver was. Since she had
come to Hallam she had only noticed him now and then
—when he drove her to the station when her mother
died, for example. He had none of the physical glamour
of his brother Will. He was of medium height, rather
overweight, with brown hair and slightly anonymous features. The school swot, grown up—or if not the swot, the
plodder. But perhaps that was just in comparison with
the other Hallams. And how many other young men
would volunteer to go and comfort a bereaved mother in
the village? How many would remember that she would
want to have the house straight when he called? It was
something she herself would probably not have thought

of. The whole expedition was a piece of quite extraordinary goodness. "Oliver is the best of us," Will said to Sarah, when they met in the early years of the war. "I know," Sarah replied.

"I suppose," said Sarah now, uncertainly, "that it's really the vicar's job . . ."

"The vicar is bedridden, and wasn't much use before. It won't have escaped your notice, I suppose, that we're not a very churchy family."

"It is one of the things that has most endeared you to me," said Sarah demurely. "Though it does rather take the shape out of the week."

"It's the *Observer* that gives shape to our week—dateline for copy, then its delivery. But if you don't believe in the efficacy of the Church, you have to take something of its function on your own shoulders. I only wish I could perform it better . . . Oh, there's Roland Bradberry. Isn't he a boyfriend of yours?"

"Just a friend," countered Sarah, but she raised her hand readily to the figure coming from the other end of the Chowton main street. The two Oxford men greeted each other warmly—a greeting in which Sarah could detect little of English reserve or of class divide. Then Oliver made his excuses.

"I must off to Mrs. Keene. See you at our first meeting of the League of Nations committee."

"Groan, groan—committees," said Roland.

"Groan, groan—Oxford!" said Oliver, turning to grimace.

"Oh," said Roland, turning back to Sarah. "I didn't know he felt like that."

"Nor did I. Maybe it's because it's his Finals year."

"I always imagined he would just coast through

them. The Hallams have that sort of reputation. All the great prizes of life scattered in their laps.

> 'We had intended you to be
> The next prime minister but three'

—that sort of thing."

"Maybe Oxford seems in some way irrelevant to Oliver, after what has happened."

"Oh God, yes. I was really shocked when I heard. I should have said something to him, but I couldn't think of anything that wouldn't sound trite . . . Did I hear him say he was going to Mrs. Keene's?"

"Yes. It's very good of him."

Roland opened his mouth, and then shut it again.

"What were you going to say?"

"Nothing."

"Don't be silly, Roland. I could see you were."

He was a very decisive young man, but he became suddenly hesitant, almost shuffling, as they stood there in the centre of the village.

"I was just going to say . . . that I wasn't sure that was wise . . . That it might be better . . . if the Hallams laid low for a while."

Sarah stared at him in outraged disbelief.

There were voices on the other side of the cottage door. Oliver hesitated when he came up to it, then knocked louder than he otherwise would. There was an immediate silence on the other side, then a firm "Come in."

Oliver ducked his head as he lifted the latch and went through the front door. It opened straight into the room that served Mrs. Keene as kitchen and dining-room. It was a room that was warm with fire and humans and animals. On the hob a kettle was beginning to sing. It should have been a happy, hospitable scene, but the two women seated at the table did not make it so. Mrs. Keene, as Oliver had said, was a comfortable figure, but, though she was dry-eyed, her mouth was set in a downward curve of pain. Her friend—in an old dress and apron, like Mrs. Keene—looked at Oliver with a sourness that amounted to hostility.

"Mrs. Keene . . . Mrs. Dunnock, isn't it? . . . I felt I had to come and say how sorry we all are about Christopher's death . . ."

Oliver was conscious, when he faltered to a full stop, that he was expecting Mrs. Keene to say how kind it was of him to come, perhaps how much she appreciated it. Awful of him, but there it was. Instead there was silence in the stuffy little room until Mrs. Keene, seeming to pull herself together with an effort, said:

"Well . . . I'm not saying *you* haven't been good to me, Mr. Oliver. You've helped, and I've welcomed your help."

Mrs. Dunnock, gazing dourly down at the table, with its check cloth and cups waiting to be filled, muttered something that Oliver, to his horror, decided was: "They ought to be ashamed."

"I hope you're beginning to get over this now," Oliver stumbled on. "This must have hit you very hard."

"I spent all my tears when my husband was gassed," said Mrs. Keene. "I've had to be hard since then."

"We were all very upset for you. Particularly as it happened at Hallam . . ."

It was patently the wrong thing to say. Oliver realized that as soon as the words began to issue from his mouth. He felt painfully his youth.

"Well, you *would* be upset!" Mrs. Keene was now

openly combative. "Very inconvenient for you! But I'm not going to apologize for him being there."

"Mrs. Keene, I didn't mean—"

"He was a good lad, and a bright one. I'm not saying he didn't get up to some silly tricks, and do things I wouldn't go along with. But he didn't deserve this."

"Oh *course* he didn't, Mrs. Keene. We all feel that."

"Oh, do you? Well, that's nice to hear, and I wish I could believe it."

Now Mrs. Dunnock showed herself as the real trouble-maker, the stirrer of resentment. She raised her head and said with deadly explicitness this time: "They ought to be ashamed."

Oliver looked from one woman to the other.

"Mrs. Keene, you surely can't think—"

He spluttered to a halt, and there was a moment's silence in the hot kitchen.

"What can't I think, Mr. Oliver?"

"That one of us . . . killed your son."

A lifetime of deference to the family at The Hall reasserted itself. Mrs. Keene, like Mrs. Battley, had been glad, on occasion, to stand in for the regular cleaning women at Hallam, and had in truth never received anything but kindness while she was there. Bringing her implied accusation out into the open put her on the defensive. She looked down at the tablecloth.

"What else am I to think?" she muttered.

"Mrs. Keene—we were all away from Hallam, at a party."

"We know all about the silly doings at Beecham," said Mrs. Dunnock. "It's less than a mile by them lanes."

"And it's news to me anyone knows *when* my Chris was killed," said Mrs. Keene, regaining spirit with the support of her friend. "They do say you was all home by midnight."

"Mrs. Keene, do please think. Think what my father and mother have done for peace. All their lives devoted to it. Have they—have any of us—ever struck you as violent people?"

"As to that, I wouldn't know. My Chris thought all that was unpatriotic, and I don't know as he wasn't right. My husband wasn't afraid to fight for his country. There's others who couldn't say the same. And there's some as would be scared stiff in a battle but mightn't be averse to killing if there was no risk to themselves . . ."

"Mrs. Keene, you *can't*—"

"Can't I? All I know is, my boy was playing pranks on your family. I don't excuse him, but he paid heavily, didn't he? You can't pay heavier than he did. And I ask myself: who else had cause to kill my Chris? Answer me that. Who else would go and do it?"

Sarah was sorry her meeting with Roland went the way it did. When they were on the verge of a quarrel she realized just how much she liked and respected him, and pulled herself back. They spent some minutes retreating and patching-up, and by the time they parted she had promised to investigate the possibility of having a day in Oxford some time during the next eight weeks of term-time. Away from Chowton they would surely be able to put the murder out of their minds for a bit.

Cards were to be had in the all-purpose shop whose Happy Families packs Chloe had so approved of. It was primarily a newsagent's, and on the counter were two or three copies of the *Daily Express,* the *Mail* and the *Herald.* Sarah wondered whether any of them had reports on the murder at Hallam. She suspected it had not, fortunately, caught the popular imagination. There had been virtually nothing in the *Manchester Guardian*.

"Cards," she said, smiling at the proprietor, and went over to the rack where they were displayed.

It suddenly struck her that she would have to write to her father. She had written briefly after she got back to Hallam, hoping the new domestic arrangements were working out satisfactorily. Since, she had not written at all. It was like sending thought into a void down a black, bottomless well. But now, if he had not read about the death at Hallam, somebody would have told him. Villages were like that the world over. And he would be worried . . . Or feel that he *ought* to be worried?

Sarah repressed the thought. No doubt her father loved her in his way. But it was not a way to evoke any response in the object.

She was conscious of being watched. As she flicked through the cheap and inappropriately sentimental cards, she knew that eyes were boring into her. She covertly looked up, into a mirror on the wall that advertised Gold Flake cigarettes. The man had his hands resting palms down on the counter, and he was regarding her with a faint, unpleasant smile which played around his lips as if he was relishing something. He was meagre of body, sunken of face, his hair was over-long and unwashed, and his jowls were shadowed with stubble.

Sarah bent her eyes back to her task. She found a card which kept its feet on the ground emotionally, though its metrical feet were distinctly wobbly. Her father would not notice this: he had no feeling for poetry. He read the Psalms as if they were *Times* leaders. She took the card briskly over to the counter and began rummaging in her purse.

"That'll be twopence ha'penny, miss."

Unluckily she had nothing less than sixpence. The man took it meditatively, and was in no hurry to put it in his till.

"Got trouble up at the Hall, ha'n't you, miss? So it says in the papers."

He gestured towards the popular dailies on his counter.

"I'm sure you had no need to wait for the papers to hear about it," said Sarah shortly.

"Ah, but we associate the Hallams with newspapers," the man said, with a shaft of cunning in his eyes. "It's how we learn their fine notions, reading them in the papers." He put the coin with infuriating deliberation into the till, and began to count out threepence ha'penny. "Funny sort of accident," he said, as he put it into Sarah's outstretched hand. "Unlucky with guns, Mr. Hallam always was."

And he snickered into her face.

Later in life, as the wife of a top civil servant, Sarah gained great expertise in how to deal with all varieties of brashness and impertinence. At twenty she had no such armoury to protect her. She gazed at him speechless for a second, then turned and ran from the shop.

"It was absolutely horrifying," said Oliver.

Sarah had waited for him on the stile beside the road that led from Chowton to Hallam. She could see as he came up that he was shattered.

"She blames us, that's clear," he went on. "But, not only that: she thinks one of us is guilty. She—and her friend—made that quite clear."

"But why? What are her reasons?"

"The same as Father gave when he said we had to be counted as suspects. We were having pranks played on

us, and we fought back. The way she put it made it sound
particularly vicious: a punishment out of all proportion
to the offence. When I offered her our help she practically
exploded."

"Of course she's his mother," hinted Sarah.

"Yes. I should have realized how bitter she would be.
The bitterness seemed to be fuelled by that friend of hers,
Mrs. Dunnock, who was with her. Please God they are
alone."

"I . . . I don't think they are," said Sarah. Hesitantly she told him what had happened in the newsagent's. She found she could tell Oliver, though she knew
she would never be able to tell Dennis. She shrank from
the look of pain and betrayal she would encounter. Even
now she found she could not ask Oliver what precisely
the man had meant. When she had finished Oliver sighed.

"That's Nuttall. I've always thought him an unpleasant man. But you're right. It must be more general. I
should have known. People were twitching their curtains
to look at me as I came down the street."

"Like Chan," said Sarah. "They did that to Chan."

"Now I know what it feels like to be an outsider. But
Chan was an exotic. I'm an outsider in my own village."

"It won't last," urged Sarah forcefully. "It can't.
They'll find who did it, and it will all die down."

"Please God they do. But what if they don't? The
longer the investigation lasts, the less likely it is there'll
be an arrest . . . I only hope we can keep it from the
parents."

Sarah thought bleakly of how unlikely that was. Already Hallam had been boycotted by two of the daily
helps. That wouldn't last, probably, but what of their
demeanour when they did come? Hopelessly, with a soli-
darity born of their common experience, they jumped

down from the stile to resume the journey home. Suddenly Oliver put his hand on Sarah's arm.

"Look."

They looked back towards the main street. Inspector
Minchip was coming down it, obviously from the Police
Station. As they watched he stopped at the gate to an
unattractive little cottage.

"Major Coffey's," said Oliver.

12

———— ● ————

What else could you expect, Inspector Minchip thought gloomily, of a party where adults gathered to play kids' games, apparently to amuse a family of aristocratic halfwits?

He was gazing discontentedly at a large sheet of paper on the Souths' dining-room table. On it he had tabulated, in so far as he was able, the movements of the Hallams on the night of the murder.

Then suddenly he reversed his thought. Games, as a rule, were things that demanded the participation of several people. Would one not expect that the Hallams' time would have been amply documented by the people they had played with? Yet there seemed little prospect that this would be the case.

The people whose movements were best accounted for were the two girls. Sarah Causeley had played croquet, eaten with Dennis and Elizabeth Hallam, then played Murder. This would have to be carefully checked with the other participants to make sure that, for example, there was not a much longer gap between finishing eating and joining the Murder game than she had allowed. But Minchip shook his head dubiously: checking

wasn't going to be easy. As Dennis quite rightly said:
nobody would have kept looking at his watch at a party
of this sort.

Elizabeth had played Sardines, eaten, then played
Murder. She was best accounted for of all. She had said
there was one time, during the game of Sardines, when it
was an awfully long time—frighteningly long, she had
said—before she was found. But it could hardly be long
enough, surely?

As to the others . . . The gaps in Dennis Hallam's
evening were glaringly obvious. Even if people had seen
him wandering around during the early part of the evening, the whole period after his scratch meal with his
daughter and nursery governess was unaccounted for.

Oliver had played Happy Families with the little ones
early on, then a couple of games of draughts with someone who had vouched for this fact on the telephone. But
from then on, apart apparently from a conversation with
Lady Wadham, he had merely observed, and had had a
long walk in the garden. In the dark? said Minchip to
himself sceptically.

Conversely the first part of his mother's evening was
unaccounted for. She claimed to have wandered round
seeing that everyone was happy and occupied, but there
was so far no corroborative evidence. And she was not a
woman nobody would notice. From about nine onwards
she was playing Monopoly, and no doubt *that* could be
checked.

Considering the party was specifically a game-playing
one, the Hallams had spent a large amount of time sitting
out, or being spectators. But there again, that might be a
comment on the kind of people the Hallams were. If it
was, Minchip rather sympathized with them.

He pushed back his chair. A game was in prospect for

him too. He could no longer delay visiting Major Coffey. He looked forward to the encounter not because he expected to like or respect the man, but rather in the spirit of an angler anticipating with relish a session with a particularly tricky trout. The Major, he knew, was a man who had tangled with the police very often in the past, and had never been significantly worsened.

As he walked through Chowton on his way to the Major's cottage, Minchip noticed two of the young people he had interviewed the day before, standing deep in conversation beside a stile. The set of their shoulders was disconsolate. He wondered if they had just been made aware of the direction that the village feeling was taking. He himself had been informed of this by Sergeant South, that most sensitive of barometers. He felt sorry for the young people. He knew the dark depths and irrationality of rural passions. Fifty years ago the family at the Hall, and perhaps even their servants, would have been shielded by habits of deference. That was much less the case today. He thought cynically: I'm sure Dennis Hallam greatly disapproves of deference.

The cottage was square and unattractive, though in excellent repair. Even the front garden was given over to vegetables, apart from one or two elderly shrubs. The Major preparing to feed himself in the next war, thought Minchip. Or maybe it was just that the Major was not particularly well off. He screwed round the little handle that rang the bell, and waited.

The Major, when he opened the door, was a shadowy figure. The cottage had a poky hallway, but there was no light in it. The Major stood back to let him in.

"Ah, Inspector," he said. "I've been expecting you."

"Expecting?" Minchip queried, crossing the threshold.

"But naturally. I was at the Wadhams' gathering. And you will no doubt have heard that Christopher Keene was one of my little group."

So frankness was to be the opening gambit, thought Minchip, as he was ushered into the sitting-room.

"You will have a cup of coffee?"

Minchip had had coffee not half an hour before, but he accepted. He was willing to bet the Major employed no maid, and it would give him a chance to examine the room.

It was a larger room than he had expected. The cottage was in fact two cottages knocked together—as was usually the case when gentry bought themselves a rural retirement home. This room represented the whole ground floor of one of them. The furniture was old, angular, and—as Minchip was soon to find out—uncomfortable. Inherited, no doubt. Probably the furniture Major Coffey had grown up with. In a wooden box under the window were dumbbells and Indian clubs. The bookshelf was a meagre affair. Army manuals, books on guns and gun lore, memoirs of army men and Empire Builders, some of them personally dedicated. The only overtly political work was Herr Hitler's *My Struggle.*

On his brief visit inside Hallam, Inspector Minchip had inevitably become aware that books dominated the house. Here it was guns. He had not noticed that immediately, because Coffey had not switched on the light. The cases containing them were down the far end of the room, much in shadow, but a miniature chandelier showed that in the evening they would be the focal point of the room. There was one case attached to the wall containing rifles, another glass display case containing pistols and Service revolvers. This was not a collection of

antiques and curiosities. These were all recent weapons
that had seen service.

Minchip only had time to take in the major salient
points of the collection when Coffey came in, bearing a
tray.

"It's a dreary sort of day," he said, in his soft voice
with the suggestion of a lisp. He switched on the light.
"Ah, you are examining my collection."

"Yes, indeed. Everything except a cannon."

Coffey laughed mirthlessly.

"Do come and sit down. At least you can see that I
don't try to hide my interest in guns."

"You would gain nothing by doing so. I would have
presumed that a retired military man *had* guns. And naturally the whole village would know of your collection."

They sat down. Major Coffey poured, and immediately stood up, ranging around the room, cup in hand.
Minchip sipped at his brew. At least it was more palat-
able than Mrs. South's concoction—coffee essence with
boiling milk poured over it. He sat back in his chair and
contemplated the Major. If one looked at the figure alone
he was rather an impressive man: tall, trim, limber, up-
right. A finely preserved male animal. The face was another matter: in spite of the short haircut and military
moustache it was secretive, changeable, untrustworthy. It
was the face, Minchip felt, of a disappointed man, of one
who had always felt his merits exceeded his promotion.
Nevertheless, he had no doubt that the brain behind the
face was agile, even if it was unsound.

Major Coffey, suddenly aware he was being watched,
came and sat down.

"Good," said Minchip. "Otherwise I should have had
to stand up. I can't start the interview at a disadvantage."

Major Coffey smiled an inward, prickly smile.

"I have no desire to put you at a disadvantage. I intend to cooperate with you fully."

"I'm glad to hear it. Tell me, Major, what was the precise nature of your connection with the young men of these villages?"

The Major looked at him straight.

"You are not, I hope, suggesting any kind of moral turpitude?"

"I am not suggesting anything at all. I am merely asking a question."

"Because let me assure you, if there were anything of that despicable nature, it would have been round the village in no time."

That, at any rate, was true.

"Perhaps you would answer my question."

Major Coffey, having made his point, sat back, considering.

"The precise nature, I think you said, of my connection with the young men of the village? I think you might say that I am some kind of leader. Yes, I think you might say that. They are, as I expect you appreciate, lively, high-spirited young men, full of initiative. Well-educated, too, compared to the peasantry of my young days. As a military man it is natural that I should want to encourage in them a zeal to serve their King, country, and the Empire."

"I see . . . And what form does this encouragement take?"

"Oh—drill, target practice, field exercises. I try to fan into life any spark that suggests that any one of them has the martial spirit."

"I suppose among the signs of the martial spirit you would count initiative?"

"Oh, certainly."

"You encourage initiative and enterprise, then, in the boys. In what ways?"

"It is in the nature of things, Inspector, that initiative should be allowed to take its own ways."

Coffey smiled a humourless but self-satisfied smile. Minchip let that go for the moment.

"What would you say, sir, was the main purpose behind your encouragement of this . . . martial spirit?"

"Every nation worth its salt must be willing to defend itself." The voice had a certain ring now, as if he were addressing a meeting. "We live in troubled times, though to listen to the complacent talk of the politicians you would never think so. We are a nation under threat."

"You may be right, sir. But I'm rather surprised, if you don't mind my saying so, that a gentleman of your cast of mind should be preparing these boys to fight the present rulers of Germany."

Coffey sat up at once.

"Germany? Good God, Inspector, not Germany! Russia! The Bolsheviks! The enemy to the East!" He had leaned forward, his eyes glowing. Apparently he was confident that, as military man to policeman, he was addressing a like-minded soul. "That is the conflict I am preparing them for. That is the crusade all the great nations of Europe will have to undertake, and quite soon, too. And we shall win, make no mistake. In spite of the spinelessness of our present leaders we shall crush them. The struggle may be long, longer than last time, but in the end it too will be a glorious victory."

Minchip shifted uneasily in his chair.

"I fought in the last war, Major Coffey. Whatever else that conflict was, it was not glorious."

Coffey withdrew into his chair, and veiled the fire in

his eyes. There was no disguising his disappointment and
disgust.

"I am sorry to hear you are infected with the modern
disease of defeatism," he said sourly. "I myself went
straight from the war to trying to stop the dissolution of
our very nation itself."

"In Ireland?"

"In Ireland."

"That must have been very gratifying, sir. Though
not entirely successful. Can we get back to your encouragement of initiative in your little band of young men?"

Coffey had withdrawn into his shell.

"If you wish."

"I see no point in beating about the bush. We know
the boys who have been pursuing this campaign against
the Hallams. They are all members of your group. I believe they have been persecuting the family at your insti-
gation."

Major Coffey sat back in his chair and again looked
straight at Minchip.

"You put it too crudely, much too crudely. I made
the boys aware of the Hallams' deplorable opinions. Not
that I needed to. Their record and their opinions are all
too well-known." He leaned forward, once more seeking
to forge a bond. "Do you know the rumours about Dennis Hallam's *war* injury?"

Inspector Minchip had by now been briefed in village
gossip by Sergeant South.

"I know the *rumours*."

"The opinions they propagate, the causes they es-
pouse, are more than rumours. In any sane society they
would be shot as traitors. The nation that will not defend
itself deserves to die."

"Let's stick to the point, shall we? I'm not interested

in discussing politics with you. Because you disapproved of the Hallams' views you got up this campaign against them."

Coffey sat back once more, frustrated, in his chair.

"As I said, these are lively, independent boys. Young men. There was no need to orchestrate a campaign. I may have suggested that it would be a good idea to bring home to the Hallams the abhorrence right-minded people feel for their views."

"Hmm. I would have thought that some of the 'messages' conveyed in these pranks were rather too sophisticated for country lads. In particular the skeleton without a backbone . . ."

A steely smile crossed Coffey's face. It was a challenge.

"This is the age of the newspaper and wireless, Inspector. The country lad is every bit as sophisticated as his town equivalent, with whom I have worked for years. I think you would find your opinion very difficult to substantiate."

"Not as the boys start talking a little more," said Minchip, with a confidence greater than he actually felt. "But that is a side issue. No crime was being committed by Christopher Keene."

"Precisely."

"The crime was committed against him. That crime need not have anything to do with the campaign against the Hallams. Would you mind telling me, sir, exactly what you were doing during the course of the evening at Lord Wadham's?"

Major Coffey put his fingers together to form a pyramid.

"I have thought about that, of course. *Precisely* I certainly cannot tell you. I was primarily an observer. The whole occasion struck me as a trifle—what shall I say?—effete. Contests may be stimulating but *party games*—they are mere trifling. I watched the croquet, watched Monopoly, a new game to me. Then I walked in the garden. I felt, to put the matter bluntly, that this was not an occasion for me . . ."

It occurred to Minchip as an irony that Major Coffey and Dennis Hallam should react so similarly to the occasion.

"Why did you go? The nature of these parties is well known in these parts."

"I was asked by Simon Killingbeck."

"And that was enough? I see. Now, while you were walking in the garden, did you by any chance encounter Oliver Hallam?"

"I did *not.*"

"And you never went beyond the Beecham grounds?"

"To the best of my knowledge, no."

"Not down to the river, over the bridge?"

"*No.* Certainly not."

"Very well." Minchip got up. "Now, as to this collection of guns, sir . . ."

If Dennis Hallam had been present he would immediately have said: "The Purloined Letter!" He would probably have added: "It's great fun, but I never found that story very convincing." Minchip had not read the story, but he had no great hope either of finding the gun that killed Christopher Keene among the Major's collection. However he strolled casually over to the cases. The Major came after him.

"As a military man I am naturally interested in guns. You made the point yourself. A well-cared-for gun can make the difference between life and death."

"Quite. As a one-time soldier I appreciate that . . . That's a Lee-Enfield .303, isn't it?"

"Yes. A rifle you would naturally recognize."

"An old friend," acknowledged Minchip. "And that's another. Would you mind if I took those guns, sir?"

"I appreciate you have your duty to do, Inspector."

Major Coffey went forward to the case, but Minchip detained him by putting his hand on his sleeve.

"There seems to be a gap. There seems to be one rifle missing from the case."

Major Coffey gazed at the gap between two guns with no sign of consternation. Indeed he looked, if anything, a touch self-satisfied.

"There is. It's at my gunsmith's, for repair."

"Could you tell me the name of your gunsmith's?"

"Swettenham and Fulcher, in the Strand. I took the rifle there myself."

"Very well, sir. If you would now let me take those two Lee-Enfields, I'll be on my way."

And, bearing them gingerly with the aid of handkerchiefs, Minchip left the cottage, nodding a curt goodbye, and promising himself he had not seen the last of the Major.

It was lunch-time, and the little street that wound through Chowton seemed deserted as he made his way back towards the Police Station. He didn't doubt, though, that he was being watched—from a closer range, as it turned out, than he had anticipated. As he passed the last cottage before the little string of shops began, a head came over a garden gate.

"Is one o' they the gun that killed Chris Keene?"

Inspector Minchip paused for a moment, recalling all the village information purveyed to him by Sergeant South.

"You're Barry Noaks?"

Barry nodded, in his apparently vacant way, quite unsurprised that he should be known to this strange policeman.

"Is one of they the gun that blew Chris's head off?"

"I doubt it," said Minchip.

Barry smiled a slow, relishing smile.

"It won't be one of the Major's guns that did it. He's a sharp 'un, is the Major. Right down cunning."

"You know him well?"

"No. He wouldn't have me along with the rest." The tone was regretful, but not resentful. "But he's a crafty old weasel. An' he got those Hallams on the run."

He chuckled with delight.

"Why should you be so pleased that the Hallams are on the run?"

He chuckled with delight.

"Why should you be so pleased that the Hallams are on the run?"

"Think they're God Almighties, don't they? But they're nothing but rabbits. Throws up, does Hallam, if he sees a bit of blood."

"Ah—you've seen him?"

"Might have. You're no man if you can't stand the sight o' blood, are you? Stands to reason. A man's got to be able to fight, if he's a man at all."

Inspector Minchip realized he was hearing Major Coffey's world view reduced to its lowest common denominator. He wondered just how much Barry Noaks knew.

"You and I must have a little talk some time," he said, going on his way.

13

The Hallams were regaining a little of their old spirit. Oliver and Sarah had said nothing of their reception in the village, and the woman who had come to help with the cleaning that day kept well out of everybody's way. If Elizabeth was conscious of how the affair was viewed in Chowton, she said nothing. She was talking about her Season next year, though, and with a slightly feverish gaiety, so Sarah wondered whether she wasn't seeing her months in London as some form of escape. Oliver was pouring them all a sherry before dinner when Dennis darted over to a heap of newspapers on a side-table.

"I found something in the *News Chronicle* for the 'This England' column," he said with relish. The column, in the *New Statesman and Nation,* was a collection of clippings from newspapers, usually unintentionally comic or revealing. The *New Statesman* was very much one of the Hallams' journals, and both Dennis and Helen contributed to the book pages on occasion.

Dennis riffled through the pages of the *Chronicle.*

"Here it is. It's a letter, of course. 'What a pleasant thing it would be if all those people earning £2000 and over a year would each adopt an unemployed man and help him to preserve his sense of proportion by sending an occasional letter or an old book.' " When they had finished laughing Dennis shook his head. "My God—what sort of world do these people live in?"

"They live in the South, for a start," said Helen acutely. "We've become two nations again. Most of the people in Kent or Surrey haven't the first notion of what it's like to be unemployed in Bolton or Bradford."

"I found something for the 'This England' column the other day," said Elizabeth, "but in the . . . stress I forgot to cut it out. Lord Redesdale said that to abolish the House of Lords would be to strike at the very foundations of Christianity."

"I hope you went very carefully through the New Testament to find out where Christ extolled the virtues of an hereditary upper chamber," said Oliver, handing her her sherry.

"Redesdale's the man with all the daughters," said Dennis. "Even Mostyn says he's practically certifiable."

"Oh, by the way," said Helen to Sarah, "Winifred Hallam rang this morning while you were out. She wondered whether you'd like to take Chloe over there tomorrow. She felt it would get her away from the fuss and strain. But I though it might be dull for you, so I didn't commit you."

The phone rang in the hall, and Dennis got up to answer it.

"Actually I'd rather like to go," said Sarah. "I've been wanting to have a good look at her garden, and she's promised to show me round."

"I didn't realize you were interested in gardens. I'll telephone to say you'll come. Pinner or Oliver should be able to drive you, or maybe Elizabeth could."

"Does Elizabeth have a licence?"

"Do you have to have a licence?"

"Yes, Mummy, you do," said Elizabeth, with a grin. "Mind you, there *have* been times, but with things as they are at the moment I don't think tomorrow should be one of them."

"I'll take you, Sarah," said Oliver. "I've nothing to do except packing for Oxford."

"I'm sorry if I was a bit off-putting," said Helen softly to Sarah. "I don't quite like . . . well, to be honest, I don't quite like the way Winifred looks at Chloe. Sort of *yearning*. Silly of me, I know, but I can't help it. Somehow it doesn't seem healthy."

"I know," said Sarah. "I've seen that look. I'm sure it doesn't mean anything. She seems a very kind woman."

"Of course she is. I shouldn't have said anything . . . Who was that ringing?"

Dennis had come back from the hall, his face drawn.

"Minchip. He wants to come up and talk to us tomorrow."

"Oh dear," said Helen, biting her lip. "Perhaps it is a good thing Sarah is taking Chloe to Cabbot Hall. I suppose he won't want to talk to Sarah again, will he?"

"No," said Dennis, abstracted. "I didn't get the impression he wanted to talk to Sarah."

"Listen to this," said Elizabeth, from behind the *Daily Sketch*. " 'Lazy girls should be jogged into action by the news that the Duchess of Kent is doing her own nails.' "

They laughed, but nervously. Soon they trailed raggedly into dinner.

Dennis looked haggard next morning. Haggard but immensely handsome. Even towards the end of his life he had the same ascetic magnetism. Sarah saw him on television, walking near Michael Foot among the leaders of one of the early Aldermaston marches, and she said to her daughter:

"He's always had this wonderful and complete moral commitment. And when I knew him he was so extraordinarily handsome."

"Still is," said Sarah's daughter, who was devoted to 'thirties films, and admired Leslie Howard. On the screen Dennis marched forward with the wise and the good, and Sarah thought she could see the face of the man of forty-five, even that of the man of twenty she had never known.

When breakfast was over Dennis went to his study, but not to work. He was sure that Minchip would be early—was the sort of man who got up at sunrise, and talked about not letting grass grow under his feet. When Pinner showed him in at ten, Minchip thought the room was the most overpoweringly learned he had ever been in. The study—oaken bookcases, dark wood ceiling—housed the reference books so essential to Dennis's reviewing work, so he sat at his desk framed by the *OED, Britannica,* the *Dictionary of National Biography* and Groves, with hosts of lesser works around the walls. The picture within this frame ought to have been one of tranquil wisdom, but it was not.

"Are you getting anywhere?" Dennis asked abruptly.

Minchip sat down on the other side of the desk, and meditated how to answer him.

"I have talked to Major Coffey," he said carefully. "I've no doubt he was behind the series of pranks played on you."

"I never doubted that," said Dennis impatiently. "Though what the fool expected to achieve by it God only knows."

"It was all part, I gather, of preparing the lads of the village for the next war."

"Oh God—he's on that tack too, is he? Like that damned warmonger Churchill."

"Not quite, sir. Major Coffey sees our next enemy as Stalin and the Russians."

Dennis gave a wintry smile.

"I might have guessed that. Well, Stalin is doing some fine things, but I don't admire him with quite the fervour that Shaw and the Webbs display, so I can't say I relish being some sort of stand-in or stalking-horse for him."

"I have taken some guns from Coffey's cottage, but I have no great expectations from them. Tell me, sir, do you have any guns in this house?"

"No," said Dennis, without having to pause to think. "None at all. I don't shoot game, and I got rid of the family guns. I didn't want my children to grow up regarding the hunting and shooting of living creatures as a light matter."

"No war souvenirs?"

Dennis flinched.

"One keeps souvenirs of *happy* experiences. I do, anyway."

"I take your point, sir."

"I believe there was something you wanted to ask me, Inspector."

"In point of fact, no, sir. Not at this time. The person I wanted to talk to was *Mrs.* Hallam."

"Oh—ah—"

Minchip looked at him acutely.

"You seem to have an inkling of what I want to talk to her about, sir. You wouldn't prefer that I talked it over with you?"

"No. No, of course not. This isn't the sort of household where the husband speaks for the wife. Naturally you must talk to Helen."

But Minchip thought he had seldom seen a man more miserable.

Chloe was in most ways an admirable child. She was quite happy to be sat in the morning-room at Cabbot Hall with drawing-book and crayons. Inevitably she was a favourite with the staff, and one of the maids promised to look in periodically to see that she was all right. Sarah was not too happy when the little girl announced to Winifred that they'd had a murder at Hallam—murder was a word she'd picked up from Mrs. Munday, and she said it rather as she might have announced a cocktail party or the village fête—but Winifred smiled vaguely and talked of something else.

So Sarah and Winifred roamed the garden, talking begonias and wistaria, the horror of hydrangeas and the techniques of planning a wilderness. Most things in the garden were over, or near-over, but Winifred's enthusiasm and knowledge recreated the effect Sarah remembered from the July visit. In between they talked and gossiped, not of the murder, but of the King's Matter.

"Mostyn says it's about to break," said Winifred. "But he's been saying that for weeks. If it doesn't break soon he'll burst! *I* think it's just going to cool off, because I can't believe the King would be such a fool."

"What's she like, this American woman?"

"Very striking. Immensely smart, in an un-English way."

"You've *seen* her?"

"Just once. At the opera, when he was still Prince of Wales. He looked so boyish, beside her. She actually straightened his tie in public! People in the Crush Bar were absolutely horrified, though looked at in another way it was rather sweet."

"What I actually meant was, what's she like as a person?"

"I only know what people say. Sophisticated. Clever —as our royal family as a whole is *not*. Dominating rather than domineering. Unwise, it is said. But that may just mean she doesn't understand English ways, or think like an English person."

When they had finished their tour of the garden, and before going in for lunch, they stood by the corner of the house, in a patch of weak October sun, and Winifred asked: "How are the Hallams taking this?"

"Very well. But their nerves are frazzled. And I'm not sure that Dennis and Helen realize the full . . . implications."

"You mean the village reaction? No. Dennis and Helen are charming people, and good ones, but they don't always understand how ordinary people think."

"I only hope the village reaction will pass."

"It may. The old habit of loyalty to 'The Hall' has not entirely died. Then again, the fact that the Hallams are embarrassed about employing servants, and tend to have people in from the village part-time, means that quite a lot of people in Chowton are economically dependent on them. It's an awful thing to say, but it keeps them respectful."

"What I really hope for," said Sarah, "is an arrest."

"Oh, so do I. That would really clear things up. But Mostyn is not hopeful. He says that the longer it goes on the less likely it is to be cleared up."

"Yes, Oliver says the same . . . They'd hate that."

"Anybody would. It will hang around like a cloud . . . How long do you plan to stay at Hallam?"

"As long as they'll have me, I suppose. They've mentioned one year or two, possibly longer."

"But you don't plan to make a career of governessing?"

"Good heavens, no. There's less and less call every year for such a person. This is just while I think what to do."

"You may find that more than a year is too long. These days a woman has to decide what she wants to do and drive straight for it. My generation got the vote and then sat back and thought everything was settled. It wasn't. A woman's got to be ruthless if she's going to get what she wants."

"You don't sound like a Conservative MP's wife," said Sarah, laughing.

"I am that, but I'm not a Conservative wife. Oh—I am very conventional in most ways. I would have settled for the wife and mother role." Winifred looked at the ground. "But if the 'mother' business doesn't come off, the most interesting part is lacking . . . There's a void, a gaping hole. That's why I say to you, have a goal and go for it."

"I'm sure you're right. But of course the last thing I'd think of doing is leave the Hallams at this moment."

"Oh, my dear, the last thing I'm suggesting is that sort of treachery," said Winifred warmly. "But you mustn't go from being dependent on your own family to being dependent on another. You mustn't think because they are so charming and warm that they offer you a future. The reason I say this is because Mostyn and I have a good friend at Kew."

"At Kew Gardens?" said Sarah, her interest quickening.

"Yes. He's more or less in charge. They take trainees

there, who as part of the training do various courses—
Botany naturally, and garden planning—at London University and other places. It provides a very good ground-
ing, the best there is."

"It sounds very interesting," said Sarah. "In fact it
sounds ideal, if that's what I decide to go in for—It's all
so difficult at the moment, so difficult to think."

"It must be."

"I suppose the Inspector will be there by now."

"Yes . . ." Winifred hesitated, and looked embarrassed. "I'm afraid his visit may be partly due to Mostyn."

"To Mos—to your husband?"

"Yes. The Inspector was up here questioning us yes-
terday. Luckily Mostyn was down on constituency business. He told the Inspector that he saw Helen walking in
the kitchen garden at Beecham with Jeremy Cousins, and
I'm afraid it turned out that Helen hadn't told the Inspector that."

"Jeremy Cousins? Isn't he the handsome neighbour?
Why shouldn't she have told the Inspector that?"

"They had a brief fling, long ago. Oh, don't look so
shocked, my dear. It's long ago and long over. But they
remain sentimental friends. I think they have an idea that
nobody knows about it, though everybody does. It will be
much better if she gets it off her chest to the Inspector. It
will strengthen her alibi, for a start."

"Helen doesn't need an alibi," said Sarah stoutly.
"The idea of her struggling with a village boy on her own
lawn and then shooting him is quite ludicrous."

Winifred cast an anxious, longing look at the window
of the morning-room.

"We'd better go in and see how Chloe is," she said.

* * *

Inspector Minchip, sitting opposite Helen in her little sitting-room at Hallam, also thought it was ludicrous to imagine her struggling with Chris Keene and killing him. He thought as well that she looked quite breathtakingly beautiful. The auburn hair, the delicate, almost translucent skin, the filmy, loose morning dress—all these took Helen into a realm of womanliness that Minchip had previously only glimpsed, or read about. The idea of such a delicate creature taking on a village lout was absurd.

It was also, apparently, impossible, which from a police point of view was much more satisfactory. She had been with Jeremy Cousins throughout the first part of the evening. She was, however, finding talking about it very difficult, and from time to time she screwed up her mouth in a grimace of distaste. Minchip felt like a heavy-booted intruder.

"Yes, we were together till well after nine," said Helen, her voice low. "We are . . . very old friends."

"Maybe," ventured Minchip, trying on delicacy as if it were a new suit, "since I have to understand why you didn't tell me of this before, you could be a little more specific about your relationship? How close it was . . ."

"All the words seem wrong," said Helen, as if to herself. " 'We were lovers,' 'we had an affair'—all of them seem too brutal, too definite. For a very brief period we were in love."

"When was this?"

"At the beginning of the war. Nineteen-fifteen. I'd just had Oliver, but Dennis was away with the Expeditionary Force in Egypt. Dennis I had known all my life. We are cousins. Jeremy was . . . something new. He had been wounded at the first battle of Ypres, and was home recuperating."

Minchip said nothing, feeling that anything he could think of would be wrong. He waited.

"He was unmarried, and I was lonely. And frightened, I think. It was just a . . . a brief interlude of tenderness. There was nobody at Hallam except me and Oliver, and Dennis's mother. His brother Edward was in France, fighting in the trenches. It was a short episode—a matter of two or three months. A rather damp and cold affair, mostly in the open. But it was his only chance of happiness before he went back to the front. I know he thought a lot about it when he was back in France, but by then it was over. For a time he wrote, but he knew and I knew it was ended. I'd heard that Dennis was wounded and was returning home by sea. I'd never stopped loving Dennis. I'm afraid it's not true that you can't love two people at the same time."

"And the . . . affair has not been renewed?"

"*No.*" Helen was very definite. "When we meet we like to get together . . . to talk. Mostly about old times, really, as if we were old people. Dennis knows about it, and accepts that we have, still, a sort of bond. So does Jeremy's wife. It's probably sentimental and silly, but we always do it, whenever we find ourselves thrown together. That was what we were doing on Saturday night."

"I see. Well, I don't think I need cause you further pain by going into it any deeper. You understand," Minchip concluded, getting up, "that I shall have to check this with Mr. Cousins?"

"Yes," said Helen bitterly. "In this horrid affair everything decent and beautiful gets trampled over." She looked up and saw a pained expression on the Inspector's prosaic but well-meaning face. She dabbed her eyes and smiled at him. "Don't think I blame you because you have to do the trampling."

14

Inspector Minchip used the Chowton Police bicycle to get to Beecham Park. The bus would have put him down just outside the park gates, but the bus meant queueing in the main street, and enduring the curiosity of the villagers, barely repressed. And of course he could say nothing. He was sorry for the Hallams, was convinced that the villagers' line of argument that blamed them was foolish or malicious, but there was no way he could give them a clean bill of health. He simply did not know. So he took the bicycle, and his none-too-expert departure from the village riding it was watched by many curious and frustrated eyes.

Minchip thought Beecham Park very inferior to Hallam, which indeed it was. Hardly more than a ramshackle large house—and he suspected that the ramshackleness had been acquired during the present Lord Wadham's stewardship. The gardener, leaning on his spade, seemed more a token presence than a genuine fighter against the encroaching wilderness. There seemed neither pleasure nor profit to be gained from grounds such as these, though he noted that the grass around the house itself had recently been mown. Croquet on the lawn, he said to himself. In the dark, he added, and shook his head.

He was met at the door not by any maid or butler, but by a figure who, from its shabbiness, he recognized as Lord Wadham.

"Saw you coming," Waddy said genially.

Behind him as he led the way in he saw the figure of Josabeth, Lady Wadham, in grey flannel skirt and ankle socks. Both of them seemed innocently excited by his visit. There was an air of bumbling anticipation about both of them, as if he were some kind of school treat. In the background he sensed rather than saw the shape of two girls. The daughters, presumably. No doubt he was making their day too.

"You're damned lucky to find me in," said Waddy. Minchip had in fact saved his visit for a Friday, on the assumption that the Lords, who were apparently clearing up old business before the new session began, would have no matters of moment on that day, but he merely nodded. "Been to London," Waddy continued, with an air of consequence. "Stayed at my club all week, and attended the debates." He seemed to be waiting for Minchip to say something, and when he didn't he added: "You may have seen my name in the *Daily Mail.*"

Minchip, who had used the popular newspapers to shield him from the curiosity of the regulars at the Silent Swan in Chowton, where he was staying, was forced to assent.

"I did, yes. 'Self-control rather than birth control,' wasn't that it? Striking phrase."

Waddy puffed out his tummy.

"He's a good man, that parliamentary reporter on the *Mail,*" said Josabeth, apparently equally pleased at the publicity. "Waddy tips him the wink when he's going to say anything good."

"Two column inches," said Waddy. "As they say in the trade."

"Now, this business of the death at Hallam," said Minchip, feeling the Waddy self-congratulation had gone on long enough, and trying to inject a more businesslike note into the conversation. "There's one or two questions I'd like to ask."

"Do what we can to help," they both said, with puppyish eagerness.

"It's partly a question of movements. Major Coffey's for example—"

"Who's that? Oh, that friend of Simon's." Waddy shook his head. "Didn't see him all evening, apart from being introduced. Wasn't at my reading. Damned unsociable type, if you ask me. Military man. They're like that. The iron enters their soul."

Minchip sighed.

"So you didn't see him all evening. What about Helen Hallam?"

"What does she say she was doing?"

"I'd rather ask the questions, Lord Wadham."

"Because whatever she says she was doing, I'll back her up. Straight as a die, Helen. Incapable of untruth."

"You saw her during the evening?"

"Don't remember. But I'll back her up."

This was becoming ridiculous. Could Waddy be as infantile as he appeared? Minchip tried again.

"And Oliver Hallam?"

"*I* had a conversation with Oliver," said Josabeth triumphantly. "Such a *nice* lad."

"When was that?'

"I don't remember when it was, but we were standing

right here!" Josabeth pointed delightedly to the floor, as if that were the vital and corroborative fact.

"The time is more important than the place," murmured Minchip.

"Well, as I say I don't remember the time, but I do know we were talking about crosswords."

"Crosswords?"

"I was telling him how much better the *Telegraph* crossword is than *The Times,* and that we took the *Telegraph* for that reason, because it's silly to take a paper with a crossword you can't do."

"Don't you think the Hallams might manage *The Times* one?" asked Waddy. "They're awfully brainy."

Minchip decided to seek refuge from an increasingly surreal situation.

"I'd like to talk to your son."

"My son? Simon?"

"He's not away at school?"

"School?" said Waddy. "Good Lord, no. Left school last June. Says he wants to go into the family firm. We're keeping him here for a year or two. Ought to have a bit of fun first, eh? Mustn't grow up too soon." Minchip wondered what fun there was at Beecham. Apple-pie beds and Snap after tea. "Haven't the foggiest where Simon is," continued Lord Wadham.

"He's in his room."

The information came from one of the dark shadows in the background. One of the girls. Minchip hadn't been introduced, so he didn't know which. Even if he had been, he doubted if he could have told them apart. He sensed in their tone a desire to land their brother in something nasty. Well, if what he had heard about Simon Killingbeck was right, he would hardly be popular anywhere.

"Then if someone will take me up to him . . ."

"I'll show you up," said Waddy. "But it's all a lot of nonsense, this, you know. Boy shot himself."

"In that case, sir, we'd very much like to know what happened to the gun."

"Shot himself down by the river. Gun fell in, the boy staggered up the bank to die. Have you dragged the river?"

"No, Lord Wadham."

"There you are then. Anyway, that's what Josabeth thinks, and she's the brains of the family."

Minchip shuddered. They were about to start up the stairs when he thought to ask: "Lord Wadham, do you have any guns at Beecham?"

"Guns? One or two. Don't touch the things myself. Might go off. But my father used to shoot deer down in the West Country now and then, and my grandfather used to shoot poachers. Think the boy stole the gun from here?"

"Could be," said Minchip, who thought nothing of the sort. "May I see them?"

"Oh Lord, where are they, Josie?" He led the way uncertainly into the family rooms at Beecham, which resembled nothing so much as a junk-shop with a particularly careless proprietor. Nothing the Wadhams had ever bought or been given seemed to have been discarded, and around the various sticks of furniture and ornaments were draped pullovers and scarves, even a pair of trousers. Glasses and plates probably left over from the party were still to be espied in odd crannies. Picking their way through all this detritus of gracious living, they came eventually to the conservatory, and Waddy threw open the door.

"Here we are. Most of them will be here . . . Here's

the only one that's been used recently. Simon did a bit of shooting in August. See if he liked it. Don't think the birds had much to worry about."

Minchip's sharp eyes discarded that gun at once, as well as two guns suspended on the wall by the door. He walked over to an old wooden chest under the glass that looked out on to the kitchen garden and looked down without nostalgia on a Lee-Enfield .303. He could see at once it had recently been polished.

"I'll take that when I go. Nobody's to touch it, please."

"Gad. My old grandfather's poacher's gun. Claimed another village lad, eh?"

Minchip had had enough of Waddy. He led the way briskly back through the family rooms and up the stairs. At the top he let Waddy point out his son's room, then waited for him to go down again. Then he marched up to the door, knocked, and walked straight in.

"I didn't say come in," protested Simon Killingbeck.

"When I knock it means I'm coming in," said Minchip.

Simon had been lying on the bed, and had stood up to adopt a more aggressive posture. His face had an expression of youthful arrogance that would before he was much older become thoroughly unpleasant. Minchip did not suffer from the delusion that all bullies are cowards. He had fought the Kaiser's army. But he rather suspected that this was the case here. And a degree of uncertainty in Simon Killingbeck's warlike stance suggested that he had some feeling of being caught at a disadvantage. Since he obviously knew who Minchip was, this was promising.

"Sit down," Minchip said, gesturing to the bed. He hooked his hand round the top of a little chair by a desk, and swung it round so he could sit facing the bed. He set it down a little too close to the boy for the latter's comfort and sat facing him. "Well, you have got yourself into a pickle, haven't you?" he said to the next Lord Wadham.

"What do you mean? What pickle? I'm not in any pickle."

"Oh, but you are, young man. Associating with a man like Major Coffey? Getting involved in a killing? I'd call that a right pickle."

"I'm not involved—I don't associate—"

"You don't associate with Major Coffey? How did you come to invite him to the party here, then?"

"Oh, that . . . Well . . . He doesn't know many people round here, and he is a gentleman, and . . ."

"And he is a friend of yours."

"I've talked to him a bit. That's all."

"Been involved in those training sessions and exercises of his, have you?"

"No," Simon said, with lofty contempt. "That's for the village yobs."

"Ah—you're above that. So what did you do at these meetings? Talk of higher things? The destiny of the nation?"

"I forget what we talked about," said Simon sulkily. Then he unwisely blurted out: "At least Major Coffey is a patriot."

"As opposed to who? The Hallams, presumably?"

Simon Killingbeck sat there, saying nothing.

"So you've been involved in this series of childish practical jokes against them, have you?"

"Of course not," said Simon disdainfully. "That's village boys' stuff."

"The yobs again, eh? They did the spade work while you and the Major took care of the grand strategy, is that it? Very nice for you. Though unfortunately it does mean that the greater blame falls on the strategists, rather than the menials. What have you got against the Hallams?"

"Nothing . . . I haven't got anything against them . . ." Under Minchip's straight and surprisingly powerful gaze Simon looked down at his hands. "The Major says they're sapping the nation's morale."

Minchip gave a brief smile of satisfaction. The boy was hard, untrustworthy and sly, but he was still a boy, and he was still unsure of himself. He could not stand up for long to anyone with authority.

"Ah, so they're the woodworm eating away at the British oak, are they? And of course Dennis Hallam is a coward."

Here Simon smiled with unutterable contempt.

"He shot himself in the foot to get out of the war. Everyone knows that. Even my father, who's a half-wit, knows it."

Sergeant South had informed Minchip of this piece of received village folklore, and he had also confided at the same time his suspicions about the purpose of the rifle. Minchip felt it was hardly his place to defend Dennis Hallam, but he did say:

"Village wisdom is not fact."

"Oh, come *on,*" said Simon Killingbeck. "He didn't join up when war broke out. His brother Edward did, but he didn't. Not till months afterwards. His family wangled that he went to Egypt rather than the front, but even that wasn't peaceful enough for him. He shot himself in the foot and was invalided home. He was back by the beginning of 1916. Lucky, wasn't he?"

"Any man of his age who survived the war is lucky," agreed Minchip. "That doesn't mean things necessarily happened as the village believes them to have done. But that's not the point. The point is, you've just confirmed as far as I'm concerned what the purpose of the rifle was."

"What rifle?"

"The rifle that killed Chris Keene."

"I don't know anything about that."

"I think you do. The rifle was part of the set-up, wasn't it? When the Hallams returned from the party here, they were meant to find the skeleton laid out before their front door. And the rifle was apparently to be in the skeleton's hands, and pointing at its foot. *Memento Mori.* Or rather, not 'Remember you must die,' but 'Remember how you got out of the war.' "

An unpleasant smile crossed Simon's face.

"I expect something like that was what Chris Keene was getting at."

"You *know*. Because the rifle that Chris Keene was going to use came from this house."

That did floor Simon Killingbeck completely.

"You—you can't know that. You haven't found the rifle."

"On the contrary. I just have. I found it downstairs. I'm taking it with me when I go."

It was a shot if not in the dark, at any rate in the half-light. But it went home.

"I didn't give it to Chris Keene to play the trick. I didn't know anything about that. I only lent it to the Major for exercises. That's all it was!"

Inspector Minchip looked at him closely.

"Ah—now we're getting a bit nearer the truth. Five minutes ago you barely knew the Major, now you're lending him guns. Let's try and get this straight. How well did you know him?"

"We've met a few times . . ." This very sullenly.

"You visit him at his cottage?"

"I may have been there once or twice."

"Now you're talking like a village yob, or a petty criminal. *May* have been? You know perfectly well whether you've been there or not. How often have you visited him?"

"Well . . . Probably once or twice a week. Since just after I left school."

"Right. Stick to the truth in future, won't you? Because I will get it out of you in the end. You visited him regularly. What did you do, apart from talk?"

"Well . . . he taught me to shoot. You could probably get that from the neighbours, so it's no secret. There's a target in his back garden. He taught me to use a pistol and . . . military weapons. And we did a bit of strategic studies as well."

"I see. Did you learn to use firearms with the village boys?"

"No. On my own. Major Coffey said the usual distinctions should be observed. I did sometimes drop round on the nights they came, but I didn't talk much to any of them."

"Now, when did the Major ask to borrow the gun?"

"I don't remember exactly—"

"You remember. You've thought of little else since the killing."

"Well . . . it was about a week before the party."

"Had you asked him to the party then?"

"Oh yes. Yes, I had."

"And had he asked who else would be there?"

"Well, yes."

"And what did he say he wanted the gun for?"

"Well, for the normal exercises he went in for with the village boys. He said there were so many coming along these days that he was finding it difficult to equip them."

"And you said there were guns lying all over the place here at Beecham Park and nobody would miss them."

"Well, apart from me nobody shoots here. My father doesn't. He doesn't do *any*thing. So I thought I could just take the Lee-Enfield. And nobody would miss it."

Minchip certainly didn't believe that was all there was to it, but he merely nodded.

"Well, that's all very satisfactory. It clears up several things that have been bothering me. Oh—how did the rifle get back here?"

"What?" Simon had jumped.

"How did the rifle get back to Beecham? It's here now."

"Well, it sort of appeared . . . I mean, I noticed that it'd been returned."

"Oh, and when was that?"

"The day after—no, maybe two days after the party."

"And what conclusion did you draw from this?"

"I thought Major Coffey had returned it at the party."

"Did you welcome your guest when he arrived?"

"Well, yes—"

"And you didn't happen to notice whether he was carrying a rifle or not?"

"He could have returned it the next day. They leave this house open all the time. They've no sense of security."

"And why did you think it had been returned?"

"Well, maybe he found it wasn't needed . . ."

"And you weren't messing yourself with funk because it might be the gun that killed Chris Keene?" Minchip got up. "You're a rotten liar, young man. One day you may be a good one, when you've grown up the way I think you will, but at the moment you're a rotten one. You've had a week to think up a story, and you can't think up a better one than that. Your father would have done a more convincing job. Not that I think it's a matter of much importance. You were nothing but the stooge."

"I was not!"

"Well, that's what I think. But I'll be checking up in any case. I won't ask you if you made a note of anybody's movements on the night in question, because I don't think for a moment you'd tell me the truth. I shall certainly be checking up on your movements, though."

"I was with people the whole time," said Simon hurriedly. "First playing croquet, then in the table-tennis room."

"Yes," said Minchip. "I rather thought you would have been with people the whole time. I think you made very sure of that."

15

⎯⎯⎯ • ⎯⎯⎯

This time, Minchip decided, he would not interview Major Coffey in his charmless cottage. This time he would take him on at the Police Station. What was more, he would send Sergeant South to get him. They could walk together down the main street of Chowton, skewered by the watching eyes.

In the event the Major carried it off rather well—better, at any rate, than Minchip had hoped. There could be no comparison with the way South might march a village boy along to inquisition at the Station. Coffey bent down from his great height to make conversation with South's imposing bulk, and set his own pace for the walk which nothing that South might do could speed up. They might have been two pillars of the community discussing the problems of law and order, with Coffey very much the more important pillar of the two. Inspector Minchip shook his head. He had underestimated his opponent, and he had forgotten that his brushes with the law, during his years in London, had been frequent. Nevertheless, the whole of Chowton would now be aware that the Major was being interviewed at the Police Station, and would register how long he was kept there. That was something. Minchip did not like the influence of Coffey on the village of Chowton.

"Good morning, good morning," were the Major's first words as he was ushered into the Souths' sitting-room. "I gather I can be of further assistance."

Minchip did not look up from his notes, but gestured towards the chair on the other side of the table. The Major's lisp, he noted, was rather more pronounced to-day. A sign of nerves, perhaps? He wondered what communication the Major had had with Simon Killingbeck. He let the clock tick on, while he made a series of meaningless squiggles in his notebook.

"We've investigated—or the Metropolitan Police have —the gun you sent to your gunsmith," he said finally, looking up coldly at the Major. "It was indeed sent there well before the death of young Keene."

The Major twisted his mouth into a grimace.

"You surely haven't brought me here to tell me what I already know."

"They say they do a lot of business with you."

"Indeed they do."

Minchip sat back easily in his chair.

"Tell me, Major, how many boys come along to you regularly to play at military exercises?"

The Major's voice acquired a slight bark.

"You will not call it play, Inspector, when this country is at war."

"How many?"

The Major threw himself back in his chair with something like petulance.

"Let me see. There's a very faithful nucleus of five or six. And two or three more who come somewhat irregularly."

"Yes. That's what I thought. Because I have talked to

some of your little group, as you've probably heard. Now, Major, you borrowed a gun from Beecham Park."

"Well—I—yes. The young chap there, Simon Killing-beck, volunteered a gun from the family collection, and one doesn't want to discourage that sort of enthusiasm . . ."

"As I understood it, you borrowed it."

"And it was becoming difficult to equip all the boys who came along."

"Nonsense, Major. I've seen your collection. You could have equipped eight or nine quite easily."

"Valuable guns, Inspector. Not the thing for village lads to play around with."

"Don't treat me as a fool, Major," said Minchip, with an expression of weariness. "I do know something about guns, both as an ex-army man, and as a policeman. That is a perfectly workaday collection."

"I'm not a rich man—"

Minchip leant forward and rapped out.

"You borrowed that gun. You didn't borrow it for military training. You borrowed it for the prank that Chris Keene was carrying out on the night he died."

"No! I—"

"You're fond of accusing other people of cowardice, Major. And yet you borrowed that gun from Beecham so as to be sure it couldn't be traced back to you."

The Major rose from his chair. His voice had become a parade-ground bellow, and his lisp had disappeared.

"How dare you accuse me of—"

The Inspector rang a little handbell on the table, and Sergeant South came in and stood, massive and impassive, by the door. The Major subsided into his chair.

"I'm accusing you of sheltering behind one of your subordinates. I'm accusing you of being *directly* involved in the planning of these nasty japes. I'm accusing you of organizing them."

"I deny it."

Minchip relaxed again, back into the desk chair.

"It must have seemed like a good idea. Here was a sitting butt, the Hallam family, famous throughout the country for their zeal for peace. Opposition to their pacifist views was just the thing to unite a group such as you were setting up. And the nature of the pranks? Well, you had a group of lads poised between being boys and being men. The pranks were cleverly adapted to their situation."

"Anything that was done was done on their initiative," said the Major, with an air of intending to repeat that line indefinitely.

"I have talked to these chaps, Major, and I *know*. Because though you may have planned this last insult to Dennis Hallam with Chris Keene alone, he talked to the other boys. As you probably realized he would. These are country boys, not part of a military machine, in spite of your efforts. Chris was a bright, outgoing boy, who went along with all this because it was a bit of daredevil fun. He was the sort of boy—you chose him well—who would probably have flown planes, if it does come to another war. The danger involved would have been an attraction."

"He was a great loss."

"*You* lost him."

The Major's voice rose again in volume.

"I had nothing to do with his killing!"

"I'm not accusing you of killing him. I keep an open mind about that. I'm accusing you of organizing the foolish and dangerous escapade that led to his death. Let me tell you how I reconstruct what happened."

The Major assumed a posture expressive of lofty disinterest while the Inspector settled into his story.

"This was the culmination of a series of antics aimed at the Hallams, and the nastiest. It took up the rumour in the village that Dennis Hallam got out of fighting in the war by shooting himself in the foot. Those rumours were all the more persistent and bitter because I gather Mr. Hallam's elder brother, who was a more down-to-earth and popular figure, was in fact fighting in the trenches in France for three years before he was killed. The idea was to procure a joke skeleton—it being close to Hallowe'en —and paint out its backbone. Very subtle. Very amusing." He leant forward. "I believe you procured the skeleton."

"I did not."

"I don't think Chris Keene could have afforded such an object on a farm labourer's pay. And I can't find that he's been into Oxford, or any other town where it might have been bought. I shall find out. Anyway, the skeleton was bought, and the backbone painted out. The date was fixed for the night of the Wadhams' party, when you knew all the Hallams would be out. For the final, vivid touch you needed a gun, and that you heroically *borrowed,* so that there would be no unpleasant consequences for you."

The Major said nothing, but little beads of sweat were collecting on his forehead. Accusations of cowardice, Minchip realized, touched a raw nerve.

"I don't imagine the plan envisaged the gun falling into police hands anyway. I expect you thought that when the Hallams had driven home, got the full impact of the insult to Dennis Hallam, they would retreat into the house, either to phone down here to the Sergeant, or else to talk things over, in the way these intellectuals

have. Then the thing would be retrieved. Because they
were to be watched. That was always part of the fun,
seeing the effect. One of the earlier japes had been
watched by the perpetrator and by Barry Noaks. So
Chris Keene was to stick around. But because you
couldn't be *sure* this was how things would work out, you
borrowed the gun."

Minchip paused.

"The gun was loaded, because you always sent the
boys out on these expeditions armed. They weren't
pranks, they were forays into enemy territory, limited
engagements. Part of a military training. I hope you
warned him to be careful, carrying the skeleton *and* the
gun. I do hope you impressed that on him. Anyway, the
night of the expedition came. You went off to Beecham
Park, thus effectively distancing yourself from the operation. Chris Keene set out from home, collected the skeleton and the gun from your cottage—no doubt you have a
hiding place for the key—and set out along the river path
to Hallam. Not the road, because there was a real danger
that he might be seen. Meanwhile you, up at Beecham,
were not greatly enjoying yourself."

"I made no secret," Coffey said sourly, "that I felt out
of place, watching all those childish games."

"Different sort of childishness, I suppose," said
Minchip maliciously. "So you, bored and out of place,
decided to go and watch Keene executing your plan—
watch him from the other bank of the river. It's only
about a half a mile. You wouldn't be able to see the entrance to Hallam, where he was to place the skeleton, but
you would be able to observe him on his way there. The
General observing troop manoeuvres. You watched, I
suspect, but did not speak or reveal your presence."

The Major did not speak now. He sat there, a lean, military presence, with sweat on his forehead.

"You watched Keene leave the path, go up on to the lawns, and then decide to take a rest. You saw him lay out the skeleton in the way he intended doing outside the front of the house." Minchip paused significantly. "What happened next I'm not going to speculate on at this point. There are too many possibilities. But when it had happened, and Chris Keene was lying in a heap over the skeleton, you panicked."

"I never panic," said Coffey.

Minchip, who had seen *The Chocolate Soldier*, thought him faintly absurd. A parody soldier.

"Well, if you prefer it, you decided there was a need for prompt action. You crossed the bridge and retrieved the rifle. I think you might have taken the skeleton too, and dropped it in the river, only I suspect you were surprised by something, possibly by the dog being let out at the Hall, and barking at the intruders it sensed. Or perhaps you just decided that the skeleton couldn't be traced back to you. Anyway, you took the gun, and hot-footed it back to Beecham. There you waited for a suitable opportunity, probably when the guests were beginning to leave, and then you returned the rifle to the conservatory, wiping it clean of fingerprints first. Only you were a bit hurried over that. There wasn't the opportunity to do a thorough job. One of your fingerprints remained. I've checked it against your prints on the guns I took from your cottage."

There was a silence. It was not the silence of repose, but of intellectual activity.

"That proves nothing," said the Major at last. "I've admitted that I borrowed the gun. Whoever wiped it could have left one of my prints on it."

"Major, I am an experienced police officer," said Minchip wearily. "Don't try to teach me my job . . . Well, perhaps it is time now for you to fill me in on the bit I left blank. Tell me, please, precisely what you saw that night."

An expression of infinite contempt settled on the Major's face.

"Inspector, you have regaled me with a long farrago of conjecture and circumstantial evidence. You surely are not expecting me to admit for one moment that any of it is *true*."

"I think you'd be wise if you did, Major . . . Because I have one piece of evidence I haven't mentioned."

"Oh?" The interrogative sounded hollow.

"As I say I've talked with all the other boys in your troop. Naturally they're not at all happy with the way things turned out. I have a signed statement from Jim Fallow—one of your prize recruits, I gather, and your favourite—that the day after the killing you told him that 'the gun was taken care of.' You wouldn't say anything more, just that. So if I can't get you for murder, I'll have you on a charge of suppressing evidence, or conspiracy to pervert the course of justice. Think about that, Major!"

The Major thought. He seemed to be agonizingly considering his position. As he thought, his face began to glisten, and at times contorted itself briefly with rage or frustration. After a time he said:

"I should welcome refreshment."

"I'm sure Sergeant South could rustle up a cup of tea," said Minchip, gesturing to him, still in position beside the door. While they waited Minchip sat, his inquisitorial eye fixed on the Major. When the tea came the Major drank half of it, then put cup and saucer down on the table.

"The idea that I might be charged with the boy's murder is a nonsense," he said, in steely tones, with the snake-like lisp once again very pronounced. "There is no motive."

"None that I have discovered," admitted Minchip. "If there is one, I don't despair of finding it out."

"On the other hand, I have no more relish than the next man for being arraigned in court. And a charge of that kind would be particularly damaging to my reputation and influence."

"Certainly it would," agreed Minchip, mentally adding: "such as it is."

"I will tell you what I saw." The Major relaxed his ramrod stance, but there was no illusion of ease. He was as tense as he had been throughout the interview, so that Minchip wondered whether what was coming would be the whole truth, or even truth at all. "Much of what you said is tolerably close to the truth. I set off from Beecham shortly after nine-thirty. There was some moonlight, and I'd made it my business to know the terrain."

"Ah—you expected to go along."

"Shall we say I did *not* expect to enjoy a party at the Wadhams'? I thought I might enjoy watching Keene's efforts. I got to the bank at about a quarter to ten, and by then Keene was coming along the path on the other side of the river. He was coming slowly and carefully, pointing the gun *away* from himself, as I had instructed him to. When he came to the end of the lawn things were more open, so I could see better. He paused, and then started up the bank. Then he stopped by a willow tree— not to rest, but to reconnoitre, as he had been trained to do on such an exercise. There was no light on on that side of the house, but you could just hear a dog barking. Keene rightly delayed going on. Instead he laid out the

skeleton as he intended doing when he got to the house.
Then he took up the gun, and was about to place it in
position, pointing at the foot—"

"Yes?"

"When he was set upon—by a man who must have
been standing in the cover of the willow."

"I take it you could not see who it was?"

"Naturally not. If I hadn't *known* it was Keene I
could not have recognized *him*. In the moonlight they
were merely shapes."

"But you are sure it was a man?"

"I assumed it was. The shape was right for a man.
The fight was brief but fierce."

"Women wear trousers these days."

"Very few women in this part of the world do, I'm
glad to say."

"And in the course of the struggle the gun went off?"

"Yes. It went off and Chris fell immediately. The
other figure knelt by the body and examined it. Then it
ran away as fast as it could in the dark."

"Which way?"

"Towards the house and the proper road into
Chowton."

"I see . . ." Minchip considered. Thus far, he
thought, the Major had probably been telling the truth.
"And then you went over the bridge and got the gun?"

"Yes. And made sure that Keene really was dead.
There was no doubt about that at all. While I was taking
the gun from his hand, a dog was let out up at the house,
and I made my way quickly back across the river."

Minchip narrowly avoided saying "Panic." But there
was something, he felt sure, that the Major was holding
back on. Was it a fact, or something he conjectured?

"And you really had no idea who the attacker was?" he asked.

"Naturally not," said the Major, shrugging. "In the moonlight one would have had to have been very close to recognize anybody. I assumed it was one of the Hallams."

"O-oh! Why?"

"It's their house. It was their miserable cowardice that was being exposed."

"But they were all at the party."

"They could have made their way back as well as I. They could have expected that advantage would be taken of their well-advertised absence from the house to take further action against them. I knew that Oliver Hallam had been walking in the garden at Beecham at some point in the evening. I learnt later that Hallam himself had disappeared for a long period."

"But why would they have waited *there?*"

Minchip caught himself suddenly up. It would have been natural for a Hallam to wait near the house, but there were people who would have known that Keene would be coming by the river path.

"Ah—now I understand! You didn't think the attacker was a Hallam. You thought it was one of your boys!"

16

———— ● ————

The Austin Seven had been giving hints for some time that she was going to have one of her fits of temperament. Why are motor-cars always "she," Dennis wondered, as she spluttered again? And ships too. Were aeroplanes also female? The Austin choked, as she had been doing almost since Dennis left Banbury, where he had been buying records of the Razumovsky Quartets for Helen's birthday. She's going to fail me, Dennis thought, referring to Bumps rather than Helen. I should have brought the Wolseley.

Bumps finally gave up trying just before he got to Chowton. Dennis got out and raised the bonnet. He didn't know much about the insides of cars—got confused by talk of carburettors, and even of batteries—but he had been taught by Pinner that if one screwed this or reconnected that, the car would sometimes start. He looked intelligently at the collection of grimy innards, and worked through his repertory of cures.

After twenty minutes' fiddling, and rather dirty fiddling at that, Bumps still refused to start. Dennis realized that five minutes back on the road there was a country pub called the Lamb and Fleece. He could at least telephone from there to his garage in Wilbury. But when he got there and knocked at the back door—it still being the afternoon closing time—the landlord, when he opened it, shook his head.

"Oh no. No telephone here. You could 'a seen that if you'd used your eyes. Little country pub like this be can't afford thing like telephones."

He stood there, fat and unobliging. Dennis was forced to mutter "Sorry," and go away. He told himself as he walked back to Bumps that he had never patronized the Lamb and Fleece, so there was no reason for its landlord to put himself out on his account. He bent over the engine once more, noting that there was someone coming along the road from the village, so at least he could get a push if he wanted one.

So absorbed was he in his screwing and tightening that the man had passed him before he realized it, and was twenty yards away before Dennis decided that he might represent his last chance of a push.

"I say," he shouted. "I'm having a bit of trouble here. Could you give me a shove so I can try and get it started?"

The man turned. It was one of the farm labourers from Wilton Farm, Dennis thought. The man stood there, looking at him, deliberately creating an awkwardness.

"No," he shouted at last, brutally loud. "Push your own bloody car. I don't have no truck with murderers."

Inspector Minchip loved Oxford. To be sure there were the undergraduates, and lately an unpleasant amount of motorized traffic, but these were the inescapable crosses, and he bore them as the lover of Manchester would bear the grime or the lover of Brighton day-trippers. It was his

county town, and he felt it had associations and reverberations that no other county town could match.

He walked from the station to Balliol College slowly
and with relish, drinking in the sights and sounds. He
would have liked to be an Oxford man himself, but in his
young days boys of his class—unless they were quite ex-
ceptionally brilliant—did not go to Oxford. Not that
many did today, he thought, his observant eye and ear
tabulating the traces of class in the dress and accents of
the undergraduates he passed. Though he recalled South
mentioning that one of the boys from Chowton had in
fact become an undergraduate here.

The Martyrs' Memorial brought back memories of
more than one historical novel in which saintly and he-
roic Protestants suffered under the zealot Mary for their
faith, and he walked along the façade of Balliol, viewing
it with approval. He had heard the joke about *"C'est
magnifique, mais ce n'est pas la gare,"* and he had had
enough history, and just enough French, to appreciate it.
It was a good joke, but it lacked in his eyes aptness.
Balliol College was not like any railway station he had
seen. It was, he thought, an imposing building, and eminently suitable for a college, in its blend of palace and
jail.

The college porter, like all such, was a genius. He
rather thought, which meant he knew, that Mr. Hallam
was at a special tutorial with a Fellow of Oriel. No doubt
he'd be back soon after five. It was Mr. *Oliver* Hallam he
was wanting to see, was it? He'd understood that a Mr.
William Hallam was to have come up this term, but he
gathered he'd gone off to fight in Spain. Quite a number
of young gentlemen seemed to have taken it into their
heads to fight in Spain. No doubt the decision did them
credit. But somebody of *their* generation knew a deal too

much about fighting on foreign soil, wasn't that right? and would wait until they were sent to war, rather than rush into it.

The two men settled down to a mellow gossip.

". . . and though as far as official consumption is concerned they're all nice young gentlemen, between you and me there's a number of 'em that the word excrement would be a compliment for, if you get my meaning. But your Mr. Hallam is a nice young gentleman and no mistake—ah, there he is now."

Oliver Hallam had come through the big gates leading to the Broad, and was looking into his pigeon-hole. With a brief wave to the porter Minchip went out and accosted him.

"I wonder if I could have a few words, sir."

"Oh, Inspector . . . of course. Come up to my rooms. I'll get the scout to fetch us some tea and sandwiches."

"No call for that, sir."

"No trouble," said Oliver as they walked into the small quadrangle. "You've come a fair way to talk to me."

"Oh, as to that, the Force isn't letting me spend all my time any longer on the Chowton business. I'm here about a drug addict from Banbury who we think has come into Oxford to get money by peddling the stuff."

"A dope fiend?"

"That's what the newspapers call them, sir, though in my experience they're more pathetic than fiendish. We have to step down hard on that sort of thing in a community of young people like Oxford . . ."

They had come up to Oliver's room, a turreted affair at the top of one of the front quadrangle's staircases. Oliver ordered tea, and they made conversation about

Oxford until it arrived. The ham and cucumber sand-wiches were rather heftier than Minchip had expected—man-sized sandwiches, he thought approvingly, and he ate them with relish.

"I did have some purpose in dropping in on you like this," he said at last, wiping his mouth. He looked at the young man sitting on the other side of the coal fire—slightly overweight, kindly of feature, not yet fully defined or decided in character.

"Anything I can do to help," murmured Oliver, occupying himself with his last sandwich.

"You see, we know—or think we know, because people don't always tell us the truth—that Major Coffey left Beecham Park on the night of the party, and took the lane down to the river. He was bored with the games, and wanted to watch Chris Keene on his unpleasant expedition—which, as you all suspected, he had masterminded. Now, what he says happened next was this: he says Chris laid down the skeleton carefully where we found it, and was about to place the rifle in its hand—"

"—pointing at its foot," said Oliver.

"Ah—you'd got that far, had you, sir? Yes, indeed: I'm afraid so. Well, what Coffey says happened next is that a shape—he says a man, but I'm keeping an open mind—came from the willow tree, from behind or from within the cover of the overhanging branches, and that there was then a brief struggle in which Chris Keene was killed."

"I see," said Oliver neutrally.

"Now, so far as I'm concerned that puts a rather different gloss on the whole thing. For a start, there seems to be a strong element of accident there, certainly of unpremeditation. It was the victim who had the gun, too, not the aggressor. To my mind a *murder* charge would be quite inappropriate, and even if manslaughter is in question there would be mitigating circumstances . . . You get my drift, sir?"

"Yes," said Oliver, after a pause.

"Now, Major Coffey, I'm convinced, thinks it was one of the village lads in his troop who did it. Maybe a jape that went wrong. A bit of horseplay, to frighten the life out of him—if that's not an unfeeling turn of phrase. He knows that the standing he has in the village would scarcely survive if that turned out to be the case. Well, I've talked to these boys, and I didn't notice that they were concealing anything like that. Not that I necessarily would. These are not bumpkins—they're bright lads, the pick of the bunch. So I'm keeping an open mind on that too. Because there are other possibilities . . ."

"Yes," said Oliver.

Minchip shifted his position in his chair.

"Now, why I came to see you, sir, is that I thought you might like to change your account of what you did in the latter part of the evening." Oliver took a sip of his tea. "That account never quite made sense to me. A walk in the garden, yes. *So long a walk,* no. You'd been very conscientious earlier in the evening—seeing the young children were all right, talking to Lady Wadham, who—well, never mind what I think of Lady Wadham. Then suddenly you forget about the party and the games and take a long, long walk round and round a darkened garden (one that isn't at all attractive even in daylight). Your evening, if you take my point, doesn't hang together."

"It's what happened," said Oliver.

"So I ask myself," said Minchip, ignoring him, "whether something rather different might have occurred. One possibility is that you saw the Major leaving, and decided to follow him. Natural, in the circumstances,

after the cruel tricks that had been played on your family.
You probably thought he was up to some further mis-
chief, as indeed he was. If that's what happened, you
could also have seen what went on in the grounds of
Hallam, and you could either confirm or contradict the
Major's account."

He left a short space of silence, but Oliver said nothing.

"There is another possibility, of course, and that is
that you anticipated trouble that evening. You're an intelligent chap, and you realized that everyone would know
that the Hallam family would be at Beecham Park that
night. So it is just possible that you took the lane some
time before the Major, that you heard somebody coming
along the river path, and concealed yourself behind the
willow tree. And that you were so enraged by what you
saw that you threw yourself on Chris Keene, with the
result that we know."

This time the pause was more definite, but Oliver obviously realized he could not let it go on too long.

"No," he said calmly. "I just walked around at Beecham, as I told you."

"It was appalling," said Dennis, his handsome face positively haggard with misery. He poured himself a strong
Scotch, and forgot to offer anybody else anything. "Absolutely humiliating and upsetting. I'm a damned fool. I
should have realized."

"But, darling, how on earth could you?" Helen asked.
Her eyes, from the sofa, were of a watery brilliance.

"That innkeeper's behaviour should have told me. He
was almost impertinent. I should have realized then. The
people in the villages have never had much sympathy for
us, but they've always been civil."

"Who was this man?" Sarah asked. "The one who called you a murderer?"

"I have an idea he works for Edwards, at Wilton Farm. I think his name is Dunnock."

"Ah," said Sarah. "Mrs. Keene's friends."

"Mrs. Keene's friends?" Helen turned to ask.

"When Oliver called to see her, Mrs. Dunnock was there. She was very unpleasant."

"Oh dear," said Helen. "In all this trouble I forgot to ask Oliver about Mrs. Keene. Not that it matters. It doesn't sound as if she would allow us to do anything for her."

"What exactly did he say, Daddy?" Elizabeth asked.

Dennis took a gulp of his whisky, then realized he was the only one drinking and went over to the sideboard to pour them some sherry. With his back turned to them he said:

"I asked him to give me a shove, you see. To try and get Bumps started. And he turned and just stood there, looking at me. Then he said: 'No. Push your own bloody car.' And then he said he didn't have any truck with . . . murderers." Dennis straightened and brought the glasses over, his face a mask of pain. "It was like being . . . hit with a heavy club. I had to sit in the car to get my breath back. I just couldn't believe the words had been spoken."

"But if they are friends of Mrs. Keene—" Helen Hallam began.

"Oh, that wasn't the end. I had to walk home, of course. And that meant coming through Chowton. There weren't many people about, luckily, because it was nearly five, but the ones that were . . . looked right through me. And one man—Sid Cotton, you know, someone I've always thought a splendid chap—he simply turned round and went back the way he'd come, to avoid meeting me. It was terrible."

Elizabeth unconvincingly said: "You're sure you're not imagining some of this, Daddy?"

"Yes, yes, I'm sure . . . You knew about it, didn't you, Sarah?"

"Yes," Sarah said simply. "And Oliver knew. We decided to say nothing to you. We hoped it would blow over, though I don't think we thought it would. Not until someone was arrested."

"Of course, I've always known they had no great affection for us, for *me*," said Dennis bitterly. "The younger son who stepped into his brother's shoes. Edward would have done the Squire thing so much better: he enjoyed it, and they liked him. They wept in the village when he died. I was the cuckoo in the nest. And then there were those daft rumours about my wound." He looked at Sarah. "I suppose you've heard them?"

Sarah nodded.

"Oliver hinted something about them, after he'd been to see Mrs. Keene."

"I thought they'd been laid to rest long ago, but I suppose this business has revived them. People remember, in villages."

"Perhaps we should have fought harder against them," said Helen.

"I wouldn't have deigned to. A pacifist proving his fighting credentials? Anyway, the truth is so ludicrous they'd never have believed it. Shot in the foot by a bloody careless Welshman, who couldn't even do firearms drill without letting the thing off." He turned to Sarah again. "We were both in Cairo, as part of the Expeditionary Force preparing for the Dardanelles campaign. The care I got for my wound was hopeless, it started festering, and

I was shipped home. The Welshman survived Gallipoli, and sends me a card every Christmas saying it's wonderful how famous I've become and he hopes the wound isn't hurting. What am I supposed to do? Show the card around to prove I didn't do it myself? The whole thing was farcical—practically surreal."

"I don't think anyone who knew you would believe you did it yourself," Elizabeth said stoutly.

"But they do! They must do! That's why all the Major's slanders have fallen on such fertile ground. Of course I know they've never understood us, or what we've tried to do all these years. I remember saying as much to you, Sarah, when you first arrived. But you would think that when something like this came up, they'd stand by us, wouldn't you? Not immediately jump to the worst conclusion . . . You know, I really think that all our work for peace just confirms in them the belief that I'm a coward who shot himself to get out of the war . . . Sometimes I despair."

Helen patted the cushion on the sofa beside her, and he came to sit by her with a rueful smile.

"You bear the brunt of all my black moods," he said. She took his hands.

"We'll come through it, Dennis. We always have," she said. "Through my silly fling with Jerry Cousins, through Edward's death, through your coming home wounded and all those rumours the first time round. We must be survivors, I think. We'll come through all this as well."

"Of course we will . . . Meanwhile the business of coming through has to be faced up to, and I don't know that I'm ready for it yet." Dennis brushed the hair from his eyes, reminding Sarah very much of Will. "I was going to go up to London tomorrow, to see Victor Gollancz. You know, about the *Writers for Peace* anthology that he wants me to put together for the Left Book Club. I was going to take the train from Hatherton, but I don't think I could meet their faces on the platform. I think I'll drive in to Banbury . . . Isn't it ridiculous? I feel guilty and ashamed even though I've done nothing. It's like being a child again."

Elizabeth said: "It's Coffey who ought to feel ashamed. Even if he didn't kill him, he started it all off."

Helen said: "Please God it may all end soon. Please God they make an arrest."

Sarah remembered Oliver's words, echoed by Winifred: "The longer the investigation lasts, the less likely there is to be an arrest."

17

Sarah was having a nightmare. Except that it didn't feel like any nightmare she had had before in her short life. For a start she felt herself to be awake, and always in the past she had struggled, suffocatingly, to waken. Then, this nightmare seemed not to centre on concrete dangers or horrors—monsters, deformed men, precipices or juggernaut machines—but somehow to be about ideas, interpretations, mental states.

To be sure there were objects in it, and those objects seemed to have come together in some *Alice in Wonderland* sort of conjunction, but they seemed not so much terrifying as ridiculous. A cream cake and an old sepia photograph of cricket teams. Sometimes the photograph, in a silver-gilt frame, sat on top of the cream cake. Sometimes they seemed to dance in her consciousness in some lunatic waltz.

If she struggled she could pinpoint whence they had intruded themselves into her sleeping mind. Surely she *was* sleeping? They were associated with her first day at Hallam. They had eaten cream cake, and she had found it too rich . . . But *that* wasn't it . . . And Dennis had talked about a cricket game played just before the war,

between a team of his own friends and a team of village
men. The photograph she had somehow imagined for
herself, on the model of sepia photographs of parish out-
ings that they had had at home. She had never seen any
actual photograph of the teams at Hallam.

But it wasn't the cream cake or the photograph as
objects that were important. Some significance lay behind
them. There were questions that the cake and the photograph were trying to thrust upon her, but which she
struggled against articulating. And when they did assume
some verbal form in her mind, they seemed merely silly:
when Helen offered to go and fetch the cream cake from
the kitchen, did she know cream cakes shouldn't sit out
in the sun? When Dennis said that by 1916 only two of
the cricketers were still alive, was he talking about both
teams, or just the team of his own friends? The questions
were absurd.

But there was something behind them, some significance that would not let itself be thrust down, however
reluctant Sarah was to look it squarely in the face. It
seemed ungrateful, selfish, almost impious, to go into the
implications of the questions, and yet . . .

Mrs. Munday was very hard-worked. Pinner too, but
Mrs. Munday especially. She worked gladly, cheerfully,
with love—for she really did love the Hallams. But did
that make it better or worse? The Hallams were uneasy
with the whole business of being employers of servants.
That was why they employed daily women from the village. But wouldn't life have been a great deal easier for
Mrs. Munday if there had been a few more full-time servants? It was Mrs. Munday, Sarah remembered, who had
eventually brought out the cake.

She herself—this was when Sarah hated herself for
her selfishness—had had a wonderful feeling when she

arrived of being part of the family. And *such* a family. So warm, and friendly, and wise, and good-looking. They had treated her, always, as a *person,* not as a governess. When she had asked for time off, it had been conceded without question: whenever she wanted it, she only had to ask. But wouldn't it have been better if she had not had to ask? If they had come to some agreement about evenings off, days off, as soon as she'd taken up the position? She hadn't liked to ask too often, and of course the opportunities offered by the villages were few. She had really worked very hard since she had arrived at Hallam.

Of course she had worked with love—for Chloe, for Helen. She felt they, all of them, had liberated her. She had cast off at Hallam the small-mindedness and petty tyrannies of her home. And yet was there not a danger that she might, willingly and with love, have shaken off one set of family chains only to assume another set? Was that what Winifred, in her kind, not very articulate way, had been trying to warn her against?

How often had Helen put Chloe to bed since she arrived? How often had she seen Helen helping Mrs. Munday in the kitchen?

Sarah put those questions from her, as being too ridiculously petty.

Because the other question really was the more important. Somehow she was morally sure that Dennis had meant that only two from *his* team were still alive in 1916. Two from his world of witty, well-spoken, well-educated people—the sort of people with whom he felt at home.

The Hallam world suddenly presented itself to her as two tracts of territory, separated by a ditch. Within the inner circle were the family and servants at Hallam—a warm, beautiful, cosy community. Beyond the ditch was humanity at large, for whom the Hallams had a great, generous love, the highest aspirations. But between those two worlds were the people in the ditch: the people among whom the Hallams lived, and for whom they felt nothing. For example the people in the villages—ordinary, humdrum, inarticulate humanity.

Helen barely knew the names of the women who came daily from the village to scrub and vacuum and dust. She was always very charming to them, but she hardly knew them—what families they had, what problems there were in living on a farm-labourer's subsistence wage. Even her mother had taken more interest than that in the villagers of Stetford. Dennis knew more names, but he confessed himself unable to communicate with the local men, or they with him. Dennis lamented the terrible slaughter of the Great War, but when Mrs. Keene's husband died a delayed death from his wartime gassing, it was Oliver who had gone to help her get money for his funeral from the Foresters and the British Legion. Dear, kind, unglamorous Oliver—it was always he who shouldered the difficult tasks. And when he had gone to see Mrs. Keene after Chris's death, Helen had even forgotten to ask him if there was anything they could do.

Of course the Hallams had been embarrassed by the whole idea of being gentry, by the pattern of proprietorship and subservience that it implied. Yet they had lived the life of the gentry, hadn't they? They hadn't given it up. They had just given up the gentry's duties.

And it wasn't just the villagers who were somehow outside their vision. Helen had no sympathy for Winifred Hallam's frustrated maternal instincts. Her longing for children merely repelled and frightened her. It aroused no pity. And Mostyn they all dismissed as stupid.

Did Mostyn Hallam deserve the ridicule that the Hal-

lams served him with whenever his name came up? She
remembered them suggesting that he would hate them
arriving at Cabbot in Bumps, but he hadn't displayed any
such reaction, merely unashamed pleasure at seeing them
there. He had been perfectly amiable to a wide range of
people, something the Hallams found it difficult to be.
There were many different kinds of exclusiveness, and
Sarah suddenly realized that her Hallams were intensely
exclusive people.

It was Winifred Hallam who had discovered her passion for gardens. Helen had never probed her interests.
And Winifred had suggested a practical way of using that
passion in a future career. Sarah remembered Roland
telling her who had helped him get his Oxford scholarship: "Mr. Mostyn Hallam." And Mostyn helped him
out in vacations by employing him. Admittedly Mostyn
was the local MP, and had to curry favour. But she
didn't think Roland saw it like that. There had been an
emphasis: *"Mostyn* Hallam." Had he been trying to say
that he could have expected no help or encouragement
from the Dennis Hallams? That they did nothing for the
ordinary people in the village?

Why, when this business had blown up, had the villagers been against the Hallams right from the start? The
Major was a mere outsider—usually a figure of suspicion
in a village. His manner was not of the sort to gain him
support. His attitudes were reactionary in a way hardly
calculated to appeal to ordinary people. But they had
been, all the time, instinctively on his side. Was it because
they were instinctively against the Hallams?

There was something about the Hallams' attitude to
people, their relationships with them . . .

Chan. Suddenly Sarah thought of Chan. Had he liked
being called Chan? The name of a ridiculous Chinese

detective. She put the thought from her, despising herself. They had got on well with Chan: he had liked them, and they had liked him. Oliver and doubtless all his friends at Oxford had called him Chan. It was no different from shortening William to Will . . . Will, rather than Bill. Shakespeare, rather than Sikes . . .

There was something about the Hallams that instinctively shrugged off everything that was common and ordinary and homespun.

They could talk to Chan, because he was one of themselves—a thinking, intellectual, politically active person. They could not talk to Mrs. Keene. Only Oliver—kind, concerned Oliver—could talk to Mrs. Keene. A phrase from *Bleak House* thrust itself into her brain: Telescopic Philanthropy. The Hallams kept their eyes on the horizon, on a new and better world, but they hardly noticed what went on around their feet. There was in the Hallams, for all their high-thinking and their social concern, a sort of lack, a sort of blankness.

And they were quite unaware of it themselves. When Dennis had talked about his brutal reception in the village, surely there had been—she had noticed it, but hastily suppressed the knowledge—a note of self-pity in his voice. You would have thought, he had said, that the village would have stood by him. His better self would have told him that loyalty had to be earned. But at the crisis he had retreated into the role of squire, expecting the backing of the peasantry.

Loyalty had to be earned. But the public-spiritedness of the Hallams had spread itself too wide, had been too general or too abstract. And here at home they had not had enough love or concern to extend it to their poorer, less intelligent neighbours in the village. They had retreated into their warm little nest, the loving family circle with their devoted servants and their funny old car, and their ball-games on the lawn with Bounce.

When she thought of Bounce she suddenly remembered Mrs. Munday's account of him on the night of the murder, barking at the door and wagging his tail.

Sarah shivered, and knew she was awake.

18

———— ● ————

"Oh goody! We've got visitors!"

Chloe was a child with wonderfully elastic spirits. The house had been dismal since Dennis's encounter with Dunnock, and Sarah was not the least affected: she spent more time than she cared to admit wondering whether the new perspectives on the Hallams presented to her in her nightmare vision were a revelation or a delusion. "You were bound to fall out of love violently," said Will to Sarah, when they met during the Blitz.

Many years later, when plump, thirtyish Chloe came to interview Sarah for an article in the *Sunday Times* Colour Magazine on "Wives of the Mandarins" (Sarah had never thought of Roland as a Mandarin, and he himself defined his admittedly eminent job in the Colonial Office as "Preparing for the end"), Sarah had said to her soon after she'd sat down:

"Bloody silly subject for an article. Bloody silly magazine."

"What right have you to slander my livelihood?" protested Chloe.

"Well, *some* right," said Sarah. "You won't remem-

ber, but years ago, when you were very small, I was your
governess for a time."

An hour later they were in the nearest pub, drinking
pink gins, and Chloe was gurgling with pleasure at the
encounter.

"You're quite right. It is a bloody silly magazine," she
said. "You should hear what my parents say about it."

"I can imagine," Sarah said.

That was the beginning of their renewed friendship.

Now, in 1936, that sunny, irrepressible nature fought
against the gloom and tensions of the house, and the feeling of all its inhabitants that they were under siege.

"It's Chan!" she announced, as the visitors got out of
the car. "And another boy I don't know. Can I go and let
them in?"

"No, Chloe. You know Pinner likes to do that."

And he did. He felt it was for the credit of the house.
Sarah had to admit that much of the hard routine work
that the Hallams' servants went in for was entirely their
own choice. Chloe sat on the window-seat expectantly,
and Sarah stood in the doorway into the hall, watching
Bounce at the front entrance. *Flick* went the tail to one
side. Then *flick* it went to the other side. Something that
could only be described as a half bark. A friend, Bounce
thought, but not a very close one. When the family arrived home, or Pinner or Mrs. Munday, the tail went
nineteen to the dozen, and he barked continuously with
delight.

Chan made an exuberant re-entrance into the house.
He was wonderfully more confident with the Hallams
now. Dennis came out from the study, and Helen came
down from her sitting-room. Helen always looked quite
stunning coming down stairs, and Chan kissed her hand
("Goodness, how nice. I don't know when the last time

was that I had my hand kissed"). Chan introduced his friend, who was called Geoffrey. Geoffrey was rather overawed by the famous Hallams. He owned the car, but he clearly owned no such prestigious acquaintances. Chan displayed an innocent delight which verged on proprietorship.

"We are doing this little tour of the Oxfordshire villages, and I am saying: 'Let us call on the Hallams. Just for half an hour, not to disturb the intellectual activity.' Did you ever see so many books? Did you ever see so fine a specimen of Tudor domestic architecture?"

Geoffrey murmured that he never had.

Mrs. Munday brought in coffee and little sponge cakes newly baked, Elizabeth returned from a ride around the country lanes, and everyone was very jolly. It was like a return to times less fraught. Chan clearly knew nothing, or next to nothing, about the murder. The newspapers had lost interest after a day or two. It was decades before the popular press would seize with Australian whoops of joy on any whiff of scandal connected with someone suspected of being a do-gooder. The *Express* and *Mail* of the day were really not very interested in someone who enjoyed the sort of *éclat* that Dennis Hallam had in intellectual circles. It might have been different if he had had a title.

So Chan talked about anything but the murder.

"And you know your name was coming up two nights ago. Oh—what is happening to my verbs? This is because I am happy. Your name *came* up two nights ago. The students from overseas were invited to the Master's lodge for sherry—very English—and I was boasting to the Master of my friendship with the great and good Hallam family, as I do very often. And the Master, of course, was very impressed, as I meant him to be, and he was saying—he *said*—'What a pity that Dennis Hallam is a country gentleman. We'd offer him a Fellowship like a shot, but of course he wouldn't take it!' "

"You're making this up, Chan," said Dennis, though his face was blushing slightly with pleasure. "I'm no scholar, and the Master of Balliol knows it."

"You no scholar? You are joking, Mr. Hallam. You are a scholar in every field. A poly—"

"A polly?" queried Helen.

"A polymath. That is the word."

"I'm afraid jacks of all trades don't get Balliol fellowships," said Dennis.

"But you are wrong. The Master said there was nothing he would like better. Distinguished alumnus. Fine teacher, he was sure—he has heard you speak many times. Very good influence in the College. But I am saying, 'Why would Mr. Hallam come from his lovely mansion, with his beautiful family, and leave his peace and seclusion and his fine lawns and gardens with tea and cucumber sandwiches with his neighbours for smoky old Oxford with its factories and rowdy young men?' And the Master he was shaking—he *shook*—his head and said he was sure I was right."

"There are times when Oxford seems a very pleasant memory—" began Dennis, but he was interrupted by a ring at the doorbell. "Oh dear. I think this will be Minchip. He said he'd be coming to see me some time this morning. I've got a very good idea of what he's going to tell me."

As Dennis slipped out, some of the bloom went out of the party, but if Chan noticed he gave no sign, and he rattled on so happily that his half-hour's visit stretched out to an hour and a half.

* * *

"There's never an *end* to an investigation of an unsolved crime," said Minchip. He was being a little pedantic and policemanly, as if the study induced in him feelings of inferiority. "We don't even talk about it being *shelved.* If any piece of information comes up, say from Sergeant South or from any of the people involved, then the case will be reopened straight away. But I'm afraid I'm being taken off active investigation of it."

"So the thing hangs round our necks like an albatross for the rest of our lives," said Dennis bitterly.

"I can see you must feel that," said Minchip. "It's a blow for me, too."

Dennis was immediately sympathetic.

"Yes, of course. A blow to your professional pride—I can understand that. I must say when you arrived first, I quite expected you to clear the thing up easily."

"I don't know that I did, sir. Villages are clannish places, as I'm sure you've found, sir." Dennis nodded a heartfelt assent. "And the Major is a cunning individual, with long experience of brushes with the police. Not that I'm saying the village is shielding anyone, or that the Major is shielding anyone. I just don't know."

"The fact that Keene was the one with the gun hasn't helped, I suppose?"

"No, it hasn't, sir. If when I finally got hold of it we had found a fingerprint on it of someone whose print shouldn't have been there, that might have been another matter. But the lads, the Major, the Wadhams—all their prints could have got there in the normal course of events."

"You mean, you might have felt you were on to something if you'd found one of *our* prints," said Dennis acutely.

"Maybe, sir. But even then, I don't know how much forrarder I'd have been. You are neighbours of the Wadhams, after all. No, if I felt I was getting somewhere, was within an inch, or even a foot, of coming up with something, I'd plead for more time. But I don't. I've been in every direction: the lads—whether in horseplay, or someone with a grudge against Keene; the Major; the Wadhams, especially that young Simon; yourselves, obviously, sir . . ."

"Yes. I suppose we do have the best motive."

"You have the best motive *that I know of,* sir. And of course your accounts of what you were doing at the relevant times are not satisfactory as far as providing an alibi is concerned. One can even slip away from games like Sardines and Murder. I was interested for a time in the fact that your daughter went to the party as Orlofsky."

"I beg your pardon?"

"Prince Orlofsky from *Fledermaus,* sir. I'm rather partial to a bit of operetta. A male part, played by a woman. And the Major was convinced that the form which attacked Chris Keene was wearing trousers . . . but in any case, every avenue I've gone up has led to a blank wall. I can't in all conscience tell my Super that I'm getting anywhere. And now apparently there's been a message from Scotland Yard to see whether we can send some men to London to be on standby. Apparently they're expecting large-scale trouble, though heaven knows what kind. I've heard no talk of a strike or anything."

"Probably 'The King's Matter,' " said Dennis.

"The King's matter?" Minchip had pricked up his ears at once.

"The King wants to marry an American woman."

"American!" Minchip sat back in his chair as if

winded, but he soon thought over his reaction. "But there wouldn't be any objection to that, would there, sir? No constitutional objection?"

"Oh no. But the lady happens to have been twice divorced."

Minchip whistled.

"That puts the lid on it."

"Yes. Considering the founder of our national church divorced two ladies, and got rid of two more in very nasty circumstances, our Church leaders are surprisingly sniffy on the subject of divorce. I've no doubt if Edward does decide to put the woman before the throne, the present Archbishop will find something sanctimonious to say on the matter."

"Put the woman . . . You mean he might *resign,* sir? Abdicate?"

"I gather there's a distinct possibility. He wants to get the whole thing over well before the Coronation."

"Good Lord! Well, you have dumbfounded me! And do I gather, sir, you've known this for some time?"

"Oh yes. Everyone's been talking about it since early summer. My cousin Mostyn Hallam is always burbling on about it behind his hand. I must say I don't see it as the sort of cataclysmic event he apparently envisages. With Spain going up in flames, with a son fighting in the International Brigade, I can only see this as a very minor event."

Minchip felt reproved for his interest, but he kept his end up.

"Yes. I can see that you would feel like that, sir. I must say to me it seems like the end of an era. And the old King not dead a year." He got up. "I'll say goodbye, sir. I think I'll go back to headquarters and say I'm willing to be drafted to London. It's not often you get a chance to be in on a piece of history like this."

Dennis reflected wryly that the end of the investigation was at least bringing joy to somebody.

"Did Chan get off all right?" Dennis asked, as they sat around after lunch, drinking coffee again.

"Oh yes. They were going on to Deddington and Chipping Norton. The other boy seemed nice too."

"Interesting what Chan said," Dennis remarked casually. "About what the Master said to him. He was probably just exaggerating casual chit-chat. Pity in a way. It could be that a term or so at Oxford, teaching and writing, might be just what I need at the moment."

Helen pitched her reply equally casually.

"Why don't you give the Master a ring?"

"I might a bit later on."

When he left to go to his study they all knew what he was going to do. But he just said:

"Ah well, back to Lawrence of Arabia. Do you know, I'm receiving a strong impression that that young man was untruthful! But I suppose all hell would break loose if I said so."

He did not go back to Lawrence of Arabia. He came back into the sitting-room a quarter of an hour later, and he had a gleam in his eye for the first time in weeks.

"A great piece of luck. One of the History dons is having to take next term off—he's having an operation in the New Year. The Master has asked me to take his place."

"Oh, marvellous!" said Helen. "Just what you need."

"It should be no problem to rent a house."

"And did he say anything about a Fellowship?"

"Oh, he *did.*" Dennis shuffled from foot to foot, uneasily. "But of course it's out of the question."

Helen put out her hands to him, and once more drew him down on to the sofa.

"*Why,* Dennis? Why is it impossible? It's what you want, isn't it?"

Dennis nodded.

"When Chan mentioned it, it seemed like . . . like a door opening."

"Then why not accept, if they make the offer? You'd find the work congenial. We'd both find the people congenial."

"Dowdy," said Dennis. "Oxford women are frightfully dowdy."

"All the better, my darling," said Helen with a laugh. "A new lease on life for me! And it *is* the ideal place for our peace work, a place in the centre of things, instead of a backwater. It's a place where we'd feel at home, with kindred spirits."

"Awfully easy to get to London," put in Elizabeth. "If I'm going to do the Season—"

"*Are* you, darling?" asked Helen, turning to her.

"Yes, I am. Don't frown, Mummy. Coronation Year —it'll be frightfully exciting. I've asked Winifred to take me under her wing."

"Winifred . . . ?"

"Yes, Mummy. She's terribly kind and not too bright. An ideal combination. And not at all good-looking. I'd hate to have you as my chaperone, Mummy. All the young men would go after you."

"Well. if you've settled it . . . So you see, darling, there's every reason to go after the Fellowship, if there really *is* a possibility."

"I don't know," said Dennis, clearly attracted. "It seems like running away."

"Running away? What nonsense. We've never much liked being the Squire and his lady, have we? And I dare say we haven't been frightfully good at it. If people want to believe us murderers, staying here and being miserable isn't going to prove them wrong. Oliver can take over Hallam when he's finished with his Finals. It will suit him so well—he's always been good with the locals. And it will be a home for Will when . . . when he comes back. You really must think more positively, Dennis. It's the ideal solution."

It did, indeed, seem ideal. Sarah wondered, though, whether Oliver shouldn't have been consulted before Hallam was assigned to his care. It was possible, after all, that he had other plans. And, try as she might, she couldn't get rid of the idea that this *was* terribly like running away.

19

"You will be coming with us, won't you, Sarah?" Helen asked, when they had all listened to the King's broadcast.

The previous ten days had been hectic, but that had taken their minds off their troubles. There was, in any case, the scent in the air of a new life ahead of them. Dennis had a solicitor friend in Oxford—a contemporary at Wellington—and he had been looking into possible houses to rent for the Hilary term, and also, very discreetly, into houses that might come on to the market in the New Year. Oxford dons died off pretty regularly, and he had sent descriptions of several highly suitable houses in North Oxford.

"I really think £2,500 should do it," said Dennis. "Or at any rate £3,000. That's all to the good. Don't want to get into the hands of the moneylenders. And Oliver will need all the rents from the farms for the upkeep of Hallam."

Helen was busy with household matters. Mrs. Munday and Pinner both preferred to stay with the house, though they were both devastated that the family move to Oxford might be permanent. Pinner said he never *had* found a pub in Oxford he liked, and Mrs. Munday said she was a countrywoman at heart, though she'd be very happy to go down to Oxford to cook for them at any time they had a dinner party. It would be a bit lonely until Mr. Oliver finished in June, but there was the Easter vacation, and—who knew?—it might not be long before he found a young lady who suited him.

Elizabeth was telephoning, and going hither and thither arranging for her London Season. Coronation Year had been going to be exciting for the debutantes and their "delights" anyway, but everyone was deciding that a new king and a queen was an even better prospect than a bachelor king, particularly as there were the little Princesses, whom everybody loved. If the worst did happen, and Edward went, then the new king, whom smart society had for years dubbed as "dull," had now been found to be handsome and dedicated. His queen was pronounced to be "so sweet and pretty." It was going to be quite a season, a revival of past glories. Elizabeth made no secret of her intention of enjoying every moment of it.

Accommodation was not the only thing Dennis had on his mind.

"I think I'm going to write a book," he said. "I marvel at my self-restraint that I've never done so before. It's going to be about the Emperor Karl's peace proposals in 1916. Think of it: here was the second of our adversaries coming up with ideas to end the war. Think of all the young lives that would have been saved if the ideas had been taken up. And what did the British and the French governments do? Nothing. They simply weren't interested, though they, if anybody, knew the scale of the slaughter. It could be a very timely book indeed."

"You'll have to brush up your German," said Helen.

"I've started already. Luckily going to Wagner as

often as we do, and listening to Schubert songs, it's always there in the back of your mind. I'm surprised how much I've retained . . ."

As soon as Oliver got wind of the new plans, he came from Oxford for the day. Sarah thought that, in his Finals year, he could well have been spared such disruptions, and spared the important decisions that were being thrust upon him. Then she chided herself for the thought. Nothing the Hallams did seemed to be right with her, these days. Of course Oliver came quite voluntarily.

When he arrived, driven from Hatherton station by Pinner, she found herself watching Bounce. It was absurd, of course. Bounce stood at the front entrance, barking and wagging his tail nineteen to the dozen. That's what he did every time a family member arrived home. It told her nothing . . .

When, in the seventies, Sarah visited the house with her grand-daughter, she said to the woman in the souvenir shop that she'd once lived and worked at Hallam herself.

Oh, how interesting, the woman said. She wasn't a local herself, she came over from Banbury every day, but she did know that the last occupant of Hallam was living with his family in one of the farms.

"Wilton Farm, I think it is. Ever such a nice gentleman, Mr. Oliver, so everyone says."

"Yes, Oliver was terribly nice," the 55-year-old Sarah said.

"I'm sure he'd love a visit from you," said the woman. "For old times' sake."

"I'm afraid I haven't time today," said Sarah. "We have to rush. Perhaps next time I come . . ."

But she knew there would not be a next time, and that she would never go and visit Oliver Hallam. And she knew the reason was that she had suspected that generous, selfless man of the murder of Chris Keene.

When Oliver had greeted everyone and been to have a chat with Mrs. Munday in the kitchen, they got down to a real family council. Chloe insisted on being present, so Sarah was in on all of it, sitting with her in the window-seat, and helping her with her book.

Dennis told Oliver about Chan's visit, and his phone call to the Master. He told him about the book on the Emperor of Austria's peace proposals, and the possibility —"more than a possibility, the Master says"—of a Fellowship.

"You don't think I'm running away, old chap?"

"No, of course not," said Oliver.

Dennis explained about the house they would be renting in Oxford, and some of the possibilities if it came to their buying somewhere. He said that Oliver would have a good income from the rents of the farms with tenants, and of course the income from the bits they farmed themselves. With Mrs. Munday and Pinner staying on there would be no problems with running the house. Eventually, if things worked out as they hoped about the Fellowship, it would probably be a good idea to transfer the house to him by deed of gift, or something of the sort.

"Yes, I see," said Oliver. "Well, I'll think it over."

Dennis was visibly disconcerted.

"I say, old chap, have I been jumping the gun? We thought you'd jump at the idea—and you'll be so much better at running the place than I've ever been."

"I probably will jump at the idea," said Oliver. "But it's all new to me as yet. I'll need to go away for a bit and think it over."

To cover the slight embarrassment, Elizabeth said:

"Have you seen this picture in the *Express* of the

crowds outside Buckingham Palace? That really does look like Inspector Minchip, helping to control them."

They all agreed it did. The crowds had not been large or disorderly, and the King had been at Fort Belvedere anyway, but at least Minchip had been on the fringes of history, as he had hoped.

"He'll be happy, anyway," said Dennis. He turned to Oliver: "Now, you must do exactly as you please, old chap . . ."

Sarah had been delighted at Oliver's refusal to have his decisions taken for granted. It was a sign of his growing up, she felt. But she was not surprised, a week later, when Oliver rang and told his parents that he was quite willing to take over at Hallam when he was through with his Finals.

That made Dennis and Helen happier.

"Even after all this, I'd have hated to have had to sell the place," said Dennis.

That was on December 11th. In the evening the King broadcast—or Prince Edward of Windsor, as the meticulous man at the BBC called him. Chloe was in bed, but the rest of them, with Mrs. Munday and Pinner, sat around the wireless set, and as he talked the women's eyes brimmed with tears and spilled over.

"He was so good-looking when he was young," said Helen when he had finished. "And I do think he meant well."

"He's been brought down by the old men," said Dennis. He looked around him and laughed at their damp cheeks. "Come on—don't take it so personally. It's not any worse because he's handsome, you know. We've got a new start ahead of us too."

That was when Helen, turning to Sarah, said:

"You will be coming with us, won't you, Sarah?"

"Actually, I think I may not be," said Sarah carefully. "I've been in touch with people at Kew Gardens, and they have this scheme . . . I think it might be just the thing to suit me."

"Sarah! How enterprising of you!"

"It was Winifred Hallam put me in touch with them. Of course I'll come to Oxford for a few weeks to tide you over. But there won't be any problem finding a school for Chloe there, will there?"

"Oh no, that's quite true. There are lots of private schools at Oxford, some of them very liberal in their approach."

"I imagine the State schools are quite good at Oxford, too," said Sarah, with malicious intent. People like the Hallams did not send their children to State schools.

"We must look into them too," said Helen.

"So I thought I'd take a quick trip home for Christmas, to see if the arrangements I made are working out. I could come back on Boxing Day. Then I could help with the move to Oxford, see Chloe settled into school—" and see Roland, she said to herself—"and then, with a bit of luck, start at Kew."

"We shall be awfully sorry to lose you," said Helen. "Though in the nature of things Chloe was sure to want to go to school before long. She's a child who's made for companionship. And obviously we want what's best for you, Sarah, dear."

So the first weeks of the new reign were to be her last weeks at Hallam. It should have been a time of sadness, but it was not. She sensed new horizons, new relationships ahead of her. And in truth the Hallam that she had come to on that day in July had vanished already. Later, whenever she heard the record of Dylan Thomas reading "Fern Hill," she always shivered with recognition when he came to the bit about "the farm forever fled from the childless land." She knew exactly what he meant. The Hallam that she had come to, bathed in sun and nestled in lawns and willows, had already disappeared. It had become a mere thing of bricks and mortar, a superb specimen, as Chan always said, of Tudor domestic architecture. She had lost her adolescent illusions. She had grown up.

20

———— ● ————

The heat in the ambulance was intense, for they had been told to come as close as was practicable. Other fires, raging further down the narrow street, added to the heat and seemed likely to prevent their getting out that way. Sarah thought they would have to back into Berkeley Square, and then make their way as best they could through the cratered, lurid streets to Charing Cross Hospital. She sat in the back of the ambulance, hoping they would bring the wounded firemen out soon.

Normally, like most people involved in the emergency services, she could blot out thought. People in 1941 thought not about the progress of the war, what would happen in victory or defeat, but only about living from day to day: when they would next have food, when they would next have sleep. But in tonight's terror Sarah kept thinking: if I go my baby dies too. She kept wondering whether Roland had arrived in North Africa, trying to calculate when her letter might reach him. Perhaps in the life he would be leading a first baby would seem an unimportant matter. Sometimes it was even difficult for her, here, to think of the joy of it.

There seemed to be some movement from the blazing

building. It had been the townhouse of some aristocratic
family, converted into offices in the 'twenties. Spacious,
luxurious, heavy. The flames lapped from the windows
like the tongues of thirsty dogs. People kept comparing
the blitz to pictures by Bosch, but Sarah had never seen
any. She could only think of Milton. It was like awaking
in Hell.

Yes, there was movement at what had once been the
front door, now a gaping hole. Two stretchermen were
manoeuvring their way through, with a rough shape on
their stretcher, covered with a blanket. Behind them
came a fireman, clearly wounded, and walking un-
steadily.

"One of them's a goner," the first bearer shouted to
the driver. "Or will be before long. I don't reckon he'll
regain consciousness. The other'll be OK, but he needs to
go to hospital."

The driver nodded and started the engine, while
Sarah helped to lift the stretcher into the back and slot it
into place. This was going to be a long, slow, bumpy ride.
As she checked the clasps the other fireman scrambled
into the compartment and sank into a seat, and then the
doors banged behind them. The stretchermen ran off
down the road to one of the other fires, and the ambulance began to back hesitantly into Berkeley Square.

The fireman on the stretcher was certainly unconscious. As they turned into the square the ambulance was
in near-total darkness, only the faintest of orange lights
telling Sarah where anything was. They went forward,
lurching and hesitant, for a few hundred yards, but then
they were stopped by a small fire at ground level. Sarah
busied herself with the unconscious man, though experience told her that he was, in the unsentimental phrase of
the bearer, a goner. The whole of the bulky body seemed

shattered. She busied herself with her kit, but anything she could do was cosmetic. When the ambulance started again she sank back into her seat by his side.

"It's Sarah, isn't it?"

She jumped and stared through the flickering gloom.

"The thing about this war is, one meets just everybody," the voice went on.

She knew the voice. Oh yes, she knew the voice. And her eyes becoming accustomed a little to the darkness, she recognized with a shock that he had a nasty wound over the left eye. She imagined the red hair, the singed flesh, and the long mobile face of Will Hallam.

"It's the left side of the forehead. So appropriate," said Will.

"I started when I saw it," admitted Sarah, in a low voice. "That was my first body. You never quite get over it. Did they tell you about it?"

Will did not answer immediately, but he asked:

"How long shall we take, do you think?"

"I can't say. You must know what it's like. This is one of the worst nights yet. Do you need anything?"

"No, no . . . A bit of dressing and a good night's sleep . . . They didn't have to tell me about it. I saw it."

"You *saw* it?"

"Did you never suspect?"

In her shock Sarah blurted out something of which she was ashamed.

"I suspected Oliver. It was Bounce wagging his tail . . ."

"Poor old Oliver. Not really the temperament. He's a lieutenant in Signals, did you know? He says he's the army's most incompetent recruit but, being Oliver, he'll make himself useful somehow. The parents were very distressed when he volunteered."

"They're still the same, then?"

"Oh yes. When I was in prison in Spain they organized an Oxford boycott of Seville oranges."

Sarah bent over her patient, who was grunting in pain, then when he was silent she turned back to Will. She could see him now: still slight, but broader of shoulder; more haggard, yet somehow almost cheeky.

"I once had a vision," Sarah said. "A sort of nightmare. That your parents were not the kind, generous, high-minded people they appeared to be. That they used people, ignored the ones who were of no use to them . . . It was mean of me. After all they'd done for me."

Will smiled with faint traces of his old boyishness into her wan face.

"You fell in love with us, didn't you, Sarah? Dennis and Helen did have rather a bad habit of making people love them . . . You fell in love so completely, I suppose you were bound to fall out of love violently . . . I expect the truth is somewhere between the two. They aren't bad people, or selfish beyond the normal. I suppose the worst thing you could say about them is that they are futile . . . Dad's finished his book on the Emperor Karl's peace initiative. This doesn't seem a good time to find a publisher for it, does it?"

"I think you're talking too much," said Sarah. "That wound could turn out to be nasty."

She clasped the hand of the unconscious man on the stretcher as the ambulance lurched forward. She peered out. They were crossing Regent Street into Soho. He was a clever driver, whom the blitz had taught new tricks. He would get them there if anybody could, but by then it would surely be too late for the man on the stretcher. She wished for the hundredth time she was a doctor, not a hastily trained ambulance attendant. But she doubted if even a doctor could do anything in the present case, without an operating theatre.

They stopped in a seedy little street Sarah didn't know, behind another ambulance. She was aware that Will had been watching her, and now he started speaking again.

"Perhaps the worst thing about them, about my parents, is that they paralyse people. You can't follow that incredible mixture of public-spiritedness and personal warmth. I went to fight in Spain, and I sat on the border, paralysed. I though I'd kicked over all their training, all their oversimplified precepts, but when it came to the point . . ."

"But you *did* fight in Spain?"

"Oh yes, I fought in Spain," said Will, his voice tinged with cynicism.

"We got postcards."

"I gave them to friends who were going in. All the early ones."

"But—" Sarah wanted to put it obliquely—"how did you come to be at Hallam that night?"

Will smiled, with a sort of insolent self-deprecation that was to be his trade-mark when he hosted television panel games in the 'fifties.

"The answer is so banal that it has to be true. I was coming back to go up to Oxford. I had sat there, on the border, since August. I'd done some work with refugees, but there weren't many, so early in the war. I kept willing myself to go in, offer myself, take up the fight. And yet all the old Hallam instincts kept me there, immobilized. It was the worst period of my life . . . *till then.* In the end I could bear it no longer. I was futile, and might as well face up to my own futility. A journalist friend with the *Manchester Guardian* was motoring home. I came with him, intending to go up to Balliol, if they would still have me."

The ambulance jumped forward. Sarah saw bright firelight to her right, and realized they were going up towards Oxford Street to avoid it. They no sooner got there than they were stalled again. There was a faint sigh, but no more, from the man on the stretcher.

"Poor bastard," said Will. "His number's up."

When they had been stalled for some time, Will began again.

"This journalist was driving up to Manchester, but he made a detour and left me in Chowton. I wanted to walk, to get my thoughts together—decide what to say, how to present it. I took the river path, so as not to meet anyone. When I got to the lawns of Hallam, I looked towards the house, and there were no lights. Everyone was out."

He swallowed, remembering the time.

"I stood there by the tree, wondering whether to go and talk to Mrs. Munday. But that wasn't at all how I'd planned it. Not dramatic enough—you know what sort of a boy I was. I stood there, paralysed again. And then I heard noises from the river path. Someone coming along —quite slowly, clumsily. I couldn't imagine who it might be. I set down my haversack and waited in the shade of the willow, hardly breathing. He passed the bridge, left the path, and came up on to the lawn. Bounce had begun barking in the house. I'm sure he had sensed me there. Now there was something else too: a hostile presence. He was barking like crazy."

The ambulance was still stalled. There was a faint sound from the man on the stretcher, and Sarah took a wet flannel and bathed his face.

"It all seems so long ago," Will said wryly, as if to

himself. "Another age—when I thought the Falange taking over in Spain was the end of the world."

"And your cousin Mostyn thought the King going was the end of the world," said Sarah.

"Yes . . . Bounce quieted down a bit, and Chris Keene came up near to the tree. Now I could see who it was. He wasn't willing to go up to the house just yet. The moonlight was quite bright, and I was only feet away. I saw him smile. He put down the rifle, and then he began laying out his other burden. I hadn't been able to see what it was before, but now I saw it was a skeleton— weird, glowing. I just couldn't make out what he was doing. Then I realized there was no backbone. It had been painted out. Then, when the skeleton was tidily arranged, he took up the rifle and bent over to put it in place. Suddenly I realized what it was all about. Those rumours about Dad . . . The rifle was to be pointing at his foot. The whole thing seemed like a cruel jeer, not just at him, but at me—a comment on my funking my first test as a man, a sneer at my lack of will, my futility. I felt the blood go to my head . . ."

"We're moving," said Sarah.

"I had no idea the gun was loaded," Will said urgently, still in the past. "You've got to believe that. How could I have imagined it would be? I threw myself on him, and we grappled, and the next thing I knew it had gone off, and Keene was crumpling to the ground . . ."

The ambulance was going forward, slowly, carefully, and Sarah realized they were nearing the top of Charing Cross Road.

"That was the end of my boyhood, when I realized I'd killed him. I didn't think. I just reacted. I grabbed my haversack from beside the willow, and I ran . . . Odd, isn't it? If it hadn't been for my parents and their notions,

Chris would never have been killed. If I hadn't felt this overwhelming, crushing paralysis, I'd never have thrown myself at him. I'd have said: 'What the hell do you think you're doing?' or something like that . . .''

For some moments there was silence in the ambulance, except for the distant sound of sirens.

"Did Oliver see you?" asked Sarah.

"Oh yes. He'd followed Coffey at a safe distance. He recognized my run. Coffey saw it was a young man's run, and thought it was one of his boys. Oliver *knew* it was me. After that, all the time, he was covering up for me. He'd been suspicious of my postcards."

"Why?"

"The stories of fighting on them never seemed to correspond with the reports in the papers. He was following the war, while Mother and Father were just deploring it. Oliver is the best of us, you know."

"I know," said Sarah.

The ambulance had turned down towards Charing Cross and the hospital, but Sarah could almost feel the life of the man on the stretcher ebbing away.

"What is it Housman says gives a man the taste for blood? I don't remember, but I know killing does. It was like a release. I took the ferry to Dieppe, went to Paris, and was in on the ground floor when the International Brigade was formed. By December I was inside Spain, by the end of the year I was fighting. I fought through the spring and summer of 1937, till I was captured in October . . . I served my sentence in a Spanish jail . . .''

They were halted just above Foyle's. Firemen had cordoned off part of the road.

"I can't describe the Falange jail. The disease, the lice, the starvation . . . the beatings and the executions. Above all the executions. Everyone I knew and loved seemed to end up before the firing squad. It was hell on earth. This is heaven by comparison. I would have been shot, but I told them I was from an English noble family. They wanted to keep in with the Tories. They sent me home in March, '39, riddled with consumption . . . Funny: the Spanish war was a dress rehearsal for this one. I was in on the dress rehearsal, but missed the show. The army wouldn't have me, nor anyone else, so I joined the firemen." He nodded at the body on the stretcher. "Seems that's just as dangerous."

They were still stalled. The fire seemed to be getting out of control. Will smiled at Sarah, a smile of great charm. She was to remember it often when she saw him on television, that attractive lock plastered over his forehead, to hide the scar.

"It's odd, isn't it? I'm the only one doing something that Dennis and Helen approve of. I'm surrounded by conscientious objectors who regard my parents as secular saints. Elizabeth has married a Welsh sheep farmer and become a moral vegetable, and Oliver is in the army, as I always said he would be if war broke out. I suppose I'm happiest of all, except for Winifred, who is taking in evacuees and in her seventh heaven. Mother and Father are agonizing in Oxford over which part of the war effort they can engage in with a clear conscience."

"Did you tell them when you got home?" Sarah asked.

"Oh yes. We all went along to Minchip in Banbury, and in the end he was satisfied that it was virtually an accident. It was old history by then. Nobody wanted to revive it, and Minchip was a fair man. He could see I had suffered . . . The case is closed. Except that it changed all our lives."

The hand of the man on the stretcher went limp as

the ambulance at last moved forward. Sarah drew her hand away and looked at Will. Then she stood up and drew his eyelids down, with the calm efficiency of one who has been granted great familiarity with death.

Here's a preview of Robert Barnard's next mystery, *AT DEATH'S DOOR*, available from Dell in October 1989.

Why, Caroline wondered, do naval officers so often carry about with them a faint whiff of the bogus?

She was sipping sherry and making polite conversation about the roses with Commodore Critchley and his wife, Daisy, and all the time her mind was far away, as it tended to be on social occasions that had more to do with politeness than with pleasure.

It was true. Almost all the naval men she had known (she'd met quite a few through her father) had had it: a phony heartiness, a cultivated lecherousness, or a suspect suggestion of dreamy remoteness that probably came from reading too much Conrad. She rather thought there had been something bogus about Lord Mountbatten, and probably Nelson, too.

"Yes, we have had a vintage year, too," she said, "so I suppose I must have got the hang of pruning at last. The only thing I regret about having so many roses is the thorns. I never can teach Becky to be careful. She finds them so pretty, and it always ends in tears."

The commodore smiled a smile of studied understanding. He was chairman of the board of governors at Roderick's school. There was no particular reason for this: the Critchleys had no handicapped child, nor did the commodore show any particular interest in the children at the school or in ways of helping them and their parents cope with their disabilities. It was just that that sort of job tended to gravitate toward retired middle-class people who had time on their hands and who needed to feel socially useful. Unfortunately, the situation demanded that courtesies be shown and returned. The Cotterels and the Critchleys really didn't have much in common. Caroline particularly disliked being treated as a sexually desirable object—which she felt sure she no longer was, and certainly not to him. The commodore liked bust, and in his lady wife he had gotten it.

"At least the summer seems to be improving now," said Caroline, still on her social autopilot. "It makes such a difference if it's a bit warm. Particularly now that we can't go abroad anymore."

"Ah, yes." The commodore looked at Roderick. "Your father."

"That's right. We feel we can't leave him with anyone else—and the cost of hiring someone full-time for two or three weeks would in any case be enormous."

"Sad. Because the old gentleman lived a lot abroad himself, didn't he?" said Daisy Critchley in her metallic voice.

"Yes, he did. Particularly after the war, when we children were grown up and he had no . . . family ties. He had a flat in Highgate, and he came back there to write. I think he did that because his books were almost always set in England and he needed to be among the physical objects and the places he was describing. But he wrote them very fast, having made masses of notes while he was apparently idling away his time in Italy or wherever. And as soon as he'd finished the book, he'd hand it over to his agent, and then he'd take off again."

"I sometimes think he'd be happier now," said Caroline, "in some Mediterranean village, with some old peasant woman in black to look after him."

"Why don't you investigate the possibility?" asked the commodore.

"Because as soon as I think about it I realize that happiness just doesn't enter into it. Neither happiness nor misery nor any other big emotion. Best let him have his last years in dignity, with faces around him that he's used to."

"The feeling does you credit," said the commodore, heartily and falsely.

They were interrupted by the doorbell. Becky, who had been watching television in the corner with the sound turned downed low, jumped up and showed interest. Caroline went over to her.

"This will be our campers," she said, and she and Becky followed her husband into the hall so that they could all meet their new relations away from the hard, bright eyes of the commodore's lady.

There was time for a brief handshake all around in the rather dismal hallway that no sort of lighting could render welcoming. Caroline got no impression more specific than that of a tall boy and a short girl, both a bit travel stained. Then they had to troop back into the sitting room.

"This is Cordelia, Roderick's half sister," said Caroline brightly but casually. "And her boyfriend."

The commodore had sprung up and was doing his very-much-a-lady's-man routine, but Caroline could see the calculation in his eyes. Half sister? They had met Roderick's real sister. They probably knew that his father had been married twice, but Roderick and Isobel were children of his *second* marriage. And this young thing was his *half* sister. Then . . .

Daisy Critchley gave her husband a barely perceptible nudge, and Roderick busied himself getting the visitors drinks. Pat sat down, quite relaxed in a remote sort of way, and asked for a beer. Cordelia said she'd just have a fruit juice. Becky sat down on the sofa beside Cordelia and seemed to be quite happy, as she often was with new arrivals, just to look at her and take her in. More covertly, Caroline was doing the same. This was her first opportunity to look at the newcomer properly.

Her first reaction was one of shock, that Cordelia was not at all good-looking. Second glances made her revise that judgment slightly. She was dumpy, certainly—whereas Myra was tall, or had seemed so onstage. Cordelia's was sort of puppy fat, but retained well beyond the puppy-fat stage. Nevertheless, there was a residual prettiness in the face, plump though it was, and it looked from the faintly bedraggled hair as if Cordelia simply did not care to do much about her looks.

Pat was a beanpole boy, dark haired, with a trim beard and distant hazel eyes. It disturbed Caroline to realize that she was finally disapproving of a relationship in which the woman was the older partner. What an odd survival of popular prejudice! But Pat could hardly be more than twenty-two or -three, whereas Cordelia was certainly twenty-seven. Yet, right from this moment, Caroline sensed in Pat a sort of stillness that made him the more mature of the two.

The commodore was at his most avuncular. He was adept at small talk, and in situations like this he would use it to learn what he wanted to know.

"I don't think we've seen you here at Maudsley before, have we, young lady?" he asked, bending forward.

"No, this is my first visit."

"Then you must see plenty of Sussex while you're here, eh, Roderick? There are some wonderful walks in the neighborhood. Got a car, have you?"

"Yes—we've got an old jalopy."

"Good. Plenty of lovely drives, too. Only problem at this time of year is keeping away from the tourists. Not the best time of year to choose, frankly."

"Pat is a teacher, in a primary school. So really we don't have much choice."

"Ah yes, I see. . . . So this year you decided to visit your brother."

Cordelia flashed him a brilliant smile. It said: I know you are fishing, and I know what you want to find out, and I may decide to tell you, and then again I may not. When she smiled like that, Caroline thought, she was almost a beauty.

"I'm afraid I'm making use of Roderick and Caroline," said Cordelia, speaking tantalizingly slowly in her musical voice. "They have information, papers, that I need. . . . I'm writing a book about my mother."

"About your mother?"

Pat put him out of his misery.

"Cordelia's mother is Myra Mason, the actress."

The commodore's social manner slipped slightly. His mouth fell open. Daisy Critchley, Caroline thought, had guessed already. Now she took over, her hard social manner substituting for his well-lubricated one.

"I think Fergus was away at sea when—when there was all the talk in the papers. You don't mind my mentioning it, do you, my dear?"

"Not at all. Of course not." Caroline noticed, though, that she was fiddling with her handkerchief. Cordelia, in fact, was never still.

"Of course there is a bit of talk in the village, about the past," Daisy Critchley went on. "But Roderick's father is not really a personality to the locals. Not many of them read his kind of books. And almost since he moved here he's been . . . unwell."

"That's right," said Roderick, who had finished getting or refreshing everyone's drinks and now sat down. "It was to be his retirement home—back in England and near us. But his mind started going almost at once, and he simply couldn't cope. We moved in here to look after him. He's never been close to my sister—my other sister."

The commodore, his avuncularity restored, leaned forward and tapped Cordelia on the knee.

"I'll say this, young lady: You're the daughter of a damn fine actress. Saw her"—he looked at Daisy— "when was it? Five, maybe six years ago, at Chichester, in *Private Lives.* Never forgotten it. Or was it *Blithe Spirit* ?"

"Oh, that was *Private Lives,*" said Cordelia with enthusiasm. "It must have been eight years ago, actually. She was quite marvelous in that. All sorts of undercurrents, so you realized the play is really a forerunner of *Who's Afraid of Virginia Woolf?* I was at Kent University at the time. I went over with a group from the English Department. We were talking about it all the way home. Not often that happens with Noel Coward."

"We saw her in *Lear,*" said Caroline. "It was rather different there. She was fearsome: it was as if she were determined not to allow this appalling monster any shred of humanity."

"Yes. I remember she said that was the only way she could play her. She said the women's parts were all black and white in that play and that was how they had to be done. She certainly couldn't play Cordelia, and in fact she's never done *Lear* again."

The commodore was beginning to get uneasy with the literary talk.

"Well, you've certainly got an interesting task on your hands, my dear," he said. "It's to be a biography, is it?"

"Sort of portrait," said Cordelia.

"And you'll be here for some time, will you?" Almost automatically he ogled her. Daisy Critchley, almost as automatically, stiffened.

"I'm not sure." Cordelia, still nervously working at her handkerchief, turned with a smile to Roderick and Caroline. "I don't want to be a nuisance. It will depend on how much material there is."

"You must stay as long as you want to or need to," said Roderick.

"I fear you won't get much out of—" The commodore, unusually brutal, jerked his head at the ceiling.

"My father? No, I quite understand the situation."

"Well," said the commodore, patting his wife on the thigh, "time we were making a move. We'll hope to see more of you, young lady, if you're going to be here for a bit."

"Yes, you must both come over," said Daisy without conviction.

Cordelia reacted to the frosty invitation by smiling noncommittally and turning to say something to Becky, who was making noises. To cover any awkwardness, Pat got up, shook hands with the commodore, and made inquiries abut swimming in the area. As they moved to the door, Cordelia, perhaps thinking she'd been rude, smiled again, one of her brilliant ones, and Caroline saw Daisy Critchley realize for the first time what a good-looking girl this could be. Caroline and Roderick saw them off and into their car at the front door with the usual courtesies, and when she came back into the sitting room, Caroline said:

"And now they'll be off to the Red Lion to spread the news around the village."

"I thought they said my father was not much of a local personality," said Cordelia, sitting down again. "Why should anyone be interested?"

"Not so much because you're your father's daughter as because you're your mother's," said Caroline. "Actresses are always good for village gossip. And the fact that she's a dame will add snob appeal."

"Oh, yes, the damehood," said Cordelia.

"And the slight whiff of dated scandal will wing the story on its way," put in Roderick. "But you must know what it's like. You live in a village, don't you?"

Cordelia frowned and turned to Pat.

"I don't know. It's different. I grew up there. . . . Mother's lived there so long people sort of take her for granted. . . . Don't they?"

"Pretty much," said Pat after a pause for thought that was habitual to him. "If there's a stranger in the pub, they might boast about her. Mostly they take her in their stride."

"When I moved in with Pat, there was talk," said Cordelia. "But that was basically because he teaches in the village school. 'Can we let our innocent babes—?' You know the kind of thing. They didn't ask, 'What will her mother say?' because really my mother is hardly in a position to say anything."

"Now," said Caroline, "you're eating with us."

"Oh, no, please. I made it clear to your husband—"

"Just for tonight. I've got a big casserole in the oven. We really must have a chance to get to know each other."

"Oh, dear—we didn't want to be any trouble. We've got the Primus, of course, and we were going to have sausages and beans."

"You can have campers' food for the rest of your stay. Tonight you're going to eat properly."

Cordelia giggled.

"We'd probably have had sausages and beans if we'd been at home. I'm a terrible cook, and we're as poor as church mice."

"I noticed the second-class stamp." Roderick, turning

to Pat, laughed. "Of course, teachers' starting pay is pretty terrible, isn't it?"

"Abysmal. And I have an overdraft after teachers' college. Everyone does. It's the only way you can afford books."

"And you don't have a job?" Caroline asked Cordelia.

"A bit of journalism. I do any Pelstock story that's going for the local rag, and sometimes I do special features for them. I had a chance of getting into Fleet Street. Being mother's daughter does mean I have some contacts. But by the time the chance came up, I'd moved in with Pat."

"Never mind. Perhaps you'll get an advance on the book."

"I've had one." Cordelia grinned. "We spent it on second-hand furniture for the council house we're in. It's a bit worrying . . . in case the book isn't what they'd hoped for. Still, they tell me publishers never ask for an advance back."

"They don't usually get it, anyhow," said Roderick, who over the years had learned a good deal about publishers. "Well, that's settled. You'll eat with us."

"But we must put the tent up first," said Pat, getting up. "Easier before it gets dark."

Becky thought they were going and began making noises of protest. Cordelia bent over with great kindness and took her by the hands.

"But you can come with us, can't you, Becky? And help us put up our tent?"

"That would be kind—she'd love that," said Caroline. "There's a garden seat at the far end, near the new houses. If you put her on that, she'll be quite happy just watching."

Pat took one hand, Cordelia the other, and then all three went out to the ancient Volkswagen in the driveway. Caroline, getting the dinner organized in the kitchen, saw Cordelia take her very tenderly down to the seat. Becky gazed entranced as Pat humped the tent down the lawn, then sleeping bags, stove, and supplies. Soon Cordelia and Pat were erecting the tent with a smooth efficiency obviously born of experience.

"She's a very nice girl," said Caroline when Roderick came into the kitchen.

"Woman. Yes, she seems charming."

"I can't see anything of your father in her."

"Nor much of Myra, come to that. Though she is very pretty when she smiles."

"You noticed. She could be very attractive altogether if she slimmed and took a little trouble. Funnily enough, she reminded me of that picture of your grandmother that your father always carried around with him—probably because she was plump, too. They're both awfully good with Becky. The boy seems to have a quiet—I don't know—"

"Strength. It's a cliché, but it seems true. Whereas she —I felt on the phone, and still do—doesn't seem quite to have grown up."

"No. But remember she's had Myra Mason as a mother. Very famous, and I'd guess frightfully dominating. She probably never gave the girl space to mature, to become her own person. Children of famous people often do grow up rather inadequate."

"Thank you," said Roderick. Caroline laughed and kissed him.

"Your father was so seldom around when you were a child he didn't have a chance to restrict you," she said. "Too busy chasing his women."

* * *

The old rectory, Maudsley, was two miles outside Maudsley proper. It had originally served for the pastor to a tiny rustic church and a few agricultural cottages attached to the estate of a landed proprietor, in whose gift the living had been. Then it had been taken over to serve for Maudsley, and then, in the seventies, sold off as being too difficult to heat and maintain. Vicars, these days, were less philoprogenitive than their nineteenth-century counterparts.

The house was rambling, ramshackle, and inconsistent. The good rooms gave out on the lawn, while those on the other side were dark and poky. Only from the upstairs could one get a view of the sea. The new houses at the bottom of the garden were an eyesore, but Caroline had several friends among the women who lived there, for architectural taste has little bearing on character or disposition. On the whole she was happy at the Rectory and did not regret the decision to move in there that had been forced upon them.

The day after the young couple's arrival, while she was washing up, Caroline saw Pat setting off in the direction of the cliff path down to the beach. Ten minutes later Cordelia arrived, bursting with eagerness to get started. She had in her hand a notebook, a little set of colored felt pens, and a packet of sandwiches made with sliced bread.

"I can't wait to get down to work," she said.

Caroline took the hint and took her straight through the dismal hall to a rather inconveniently shaped room off it.

"I thought I'd put you in here," she said. "It was the room your father intended as his study, though I don't think he ever in fact worked here. He liked a smallish room, with no sort of view—nothing to distract him. He certainly would have had that here."

Cordelia looked around. On one wall an enormous

bookcase contained all the editions—hardback, paper-back, foreign—of Benedict Cotterel's works. The desk was massive, with capacious drawers, and was placed up against a blank wall. The desk calendar was for 1977. Against the wall that had a window in it—a window that looked out only on shrubbery—was a series of cupboards, old and squat.

"Now," said Caroline briskly, for she felt a certain embarrassment at exposing a father's secrets to a long-lost daughter, "you'll soon find there's very little method. I can only say that *mostly* you'll find his collection of letters written *to* him in this cupboard here. Some pretty well known names corresponded with him, and I suppose your mother's letters will be among them. His reviews, interviews with him, and so on, you'll find in these two drawers. But I don't imagine they'll be of much interest. The manuscripts and typescripts for all the books up to 1960 were bought by a university in Texas. Those for the later books are in the cupboard over there. People have started sending back either the originals or photocopies of his own letters, assuming someone, sometime, will do a collected. These we've tended to put in the desk drawers, knowing he'll never use it again. Right? That is only a *rough* guide. In fact, you'll find things in all sorts of places."

"Right . . . " said Cordelia slowly. "I'll spend the morning finding my way around. You said books after 1960 were all here, so that must mean you have *The Vixen?*"

"Yes."

"There are probably things in that that didn't get into the published text. I know my mother's lawyers were very active before it came out."

"Very probably. I remember that Ben had a whale of a time and behaved quite disgracefully. That was soon after we were married, and I was very prim, and probably too easily shocked. . . . But I must say I've always thought that book beneath him. Naked, unworthy revenge. I read it again a few years ago, and I still felt the same. I don't count that as part of his real fictional output."

"It's certainly unlike the others. Because he hadn't gone in for autobiography before, had he? Or if he had, I didn't recognize it."

"Not direct autobiography like that. One or two of his other . . . women friends claimed to recognize themselves, but they were put in plots that had nothing to do with Ben's own life."

"Anyway, that's the book that's of particular interest to me."

"Of course it is. Well, I'll leave you to it."

Caroline's day was low-key but busy. Becky had a fit of petulance and unreasonableness before lunch, as she sometimes did if she was at home and Roderick was not. Roderick was at a day-long conference of local headmasters. Caroline had a lunch of scrambled egg and fruit with Becky and Mrs. Sprigg, and when they had finished, she asked if Ben was up to receiving a visitor.

"Well, he's a bit drowsy, but it doesn't make all that much difference, does it? Who is it?"

"His daughter, actually. Illegitimate. He's never seen her before. Of course he won't know who she is."

"He won't, and that's a fact," said Mrs. Sprigg. Clearly she was interested and would get a lot more detail out of Caroline before many days were passed.

Caroline let her go upstairs to the old man, then went to the study, knocked, and put her head around.

"I wondered if you'd like to come up and say hello to Ben," she said.

Cordelia looked apprehensive, then smiled bravely.

"I'd love to," she said.

"It seemed only right," said Caroline as they went up-stairs. "Isobel, Roderick's sister, never goes to see him when she comes. But she hated him when he was—well, so in its way that's right, too."

Caroline opened the door of the shady bedroom. Mrs. Sprigg had made him clean and tidy, but already dribble was forming at the corner of his mouth. Cordelia gazed sadly at the sunken eyes, the bare skin and bone of the cheeks. It was more like looking at a skull than at a face.

"Memento mori," she whispered to Caroline.

"This is Cordelia, Father," said Caroline, bringing her forward to the bed, "come to pay you a visit."

"Cordelia . . . " said a faint, distant voice.

"She and her boyfriend are camping in the garden. It's lucky the weather's changed for the better, isn't it?"

There was a long pause, broken only by the ticking of the clock, and then the voice said: " . . . for the better . . . "

Cordelia took his hand very tenderly, then said, not really knowing what to say: "How are you feeling today . . . Father?"

There was no flicker of the eyelids. Merely another long pause.

"Father . . . " said the ancient voice.

"He's tired," said Mrs. Sprigg.

Caroline nodded, smiled at the old man, then led Cordelia from the bedroom.

"I hope that wasn't too upsetting?"

"No. I'm glad to have seen him. Is he always like that?"

"That was a bit below average. He has his good days. Then he usually dictates wills."

"Is that what the tape recorder was doing there?"

"Yes. Sometimes he doesn't remember to turn it on. He never remembers to turn it off. He leaves things he once had to relatives we know nothing about, friends who've been dead for years, people we've never heard of. As I say, those are the good days; at least it means that something is going on in his mind."

"Sad," said Cordelia. "And that's the man whose novel I'm reading." They had come downstairs, and she paused at the door of the study. "Thank you for taking me to see him. I appreciate that."

In the afternoon Becky usually had a sleep. It was a time of respite for Caroline, and as a rule she wrote letters or did anything requiring concentration. When Becky woke, Caroline took her out into the garden and did some energetic weeding. Becky watched, clutching a necklace of beads she was fond of, telling them over as if they were a rosary.

At a little after five Cordelia emerged from the house, rubbing her eyes but looking very happy.

"It's been a fantastic day," she said, coming over, "but I think I've taken in as much as I can for the moment. I'll walk and meet Pat and tell him about it. Evenings are our best times. We talk things over."

Caroline smiled, thinking it rather touching. Cordelia sat on the edge of the lawn beside her.

"I've found the most fascinating things," she said, "and learned an awful lot. You do have *all* my mother's letters to him there—first the loving ones, then the . . . the others. The last was written when she heard he was writing a book about their affair. It's marvelous—one long screed of vituperation. I can hear her saying it on-stage—hear the way she would calculate the lulls and climaxes, hear where there would be a pregnant pause. Though actually there is hardly any punctuation in it at all, as if full stops and commas would only interrupt the pure flow of vitriol. It was superb. I must take it to Maudsley and get it photocopied."

"I don't think there's any photocopying machine in the village," said Caroline. "Best to put all the things you want copied together, and then Roderick can get it done at his school." She stood up and rubbed her aching back. "Safer that way, and cheaper, too."

"That sounds ideal. I'd like the manuscript of *The Vixen* done, too, and we'd need to be careful with that. One day that will be valuable."

"Valuable? Oh, yes, I suppose an American university will buy it eventually."

"No, what I meant was, when Mother dies, you can put out the book as it originally was. Before the lawyers got on to it. Because it's got some marvelous things in it. There's a scene where he takes her to dinner at Boulestin's and she takes offense at something he says and works herself up to a tremendous scene. In the published version this becomes a quite insignificant little quarrel in the Piccadilly Lyons Corner House. It doesn't make the same impact at all."

"Well," said Caroline briskly, "I don't suppose we'll be around when your mother dies to do anything about it. And, as I say, I'd be quite happy if the book was never reprinted."

"So would Mother." Cordelia giggled. "The thing is, you can tell from the letters that the original version was the true one. There's a letter from my mother justifying herself after that scene in the restaurant. I'll have to have all the letters photocopied, I suppose. You can chart the whole progress of the affair from them . . . I calculate I was conceived during their third night together."

Caroline was a little shocked, but she shook off the emotion and laughed.

"Not all that many people can be as precise as that."

"Mother was playing Gwendolen in *The Importance of Being Earnest* in Glasgow. She came down to London on the overnight sleeper and spent the Sunday night with him. He'd been up there three weeks before, and then they didn't see each other for a month after that . . . It's funny: they're always pestering her to play Lady Bracknell now."

"Not really funny," Caroline pointed out. "Twenty-seven years have passed."

"I don't think Myra sees it like that. In fact, she always gets *very* frosty when her agent brings the topic up. But it would rather give point to the line about all women growing to be like their mothers, wouldn't it? In fact, what she *wants* to do again is her Cleopatra."

They walked toward the house, Caroline with Becky by the hand. Cordelia said sadly:

"I suppose Cleopatra really is her role. She knows her strengths. I had a real hang-up about men, you know, till quite recently. So many had come into and gone out of my life—*our* life—while I was growing up. It was Pat cured me of that . . . Funny, I used to think as a child how fantastic it would be if my father and mother met up again and got married. When I was a teenager, I used to read all his books and dream that would happen. Eventually I thought: But there's no reason why that would last any longer than my mother's other affairs."

"Your father," said Caroline carefully, "was not exactly a faithful man. You shouldn't idealize him."

"I don't. Not any longer. But I bet he was a lot of fun. Anyway, as I say, one thing I want to get is a photocopy of the whole of the original version of *The Vixen*. That way I'll know everything there is to know about my father and my mother, and their affair."

"From *his* point of view," Caroline pointed out. "Has your mother changed her mind about the affair, and about Ben?"

Cordelia laughed.

"Not a bit. She still spits fire when his name comes up."

"Then she's hardly going to want you to print any of this—her letters to Ben or the original book she objected to twenty-five years ago."

"I'm sure she won't want me to."

Something in her tone made Caroline look at her closely.

"Then you'd hardly hurt her by trying to publish them, would you?"

Cordelia's fingers were fumbling nervously with each other, but she looked Caroline straight in the eye.

"You've been very kind to me—to us. I don't want to feel I got here under false pretenses, so I think you ought to know. I loathe my mother. I hate her more than anyone on earth."